Crypsis

LM Foster

ISBN: 0615834000

9th Street Press
www.9thstreetpress.com

"Every man has inside himself a parasitic being who is acting not at all to his advantage."
— William S. Burroughs

cryp-sis *noun* - the ability of an organism to avoid observation or detection by other organisms.

I thought, since I had a few hours to kill before the killing begins, I could put it all down. Maybe when someone hears this, they'll understand the motives for the terrible thing that I have to do, and maybe it won't seem quite so terrible then. Or maybe I'll just come off as another nut. A really, really misogynist nut.

But mostly, telling the story is a way to pass the time, as I have my laptop here, and its excellent voice recognition software understands my nuances of tone, and I like to talk. Sandy used to say that I talked sometimes for no other reason than to hear myself – but that was all right with her, she'd say, because she liked to hear me, too. Then she'd laugh and kiss me.

Ah, Sandy. What happened to Sandy served to shut me up considerably. Not entirely, mind you, but I've learned to listen a lot more since then. And while I used to extol the wonderfulness of life and bless the luck I'd had in it, after what happened to Sandy, I mostly took to long silent reflections on what a shit pile my life had become.

But if I continue in this whiny vein, no one will want to hear the rest of this, no matter how much mass-murderer notoriety I accumulate. So before I detail the sad and horrible parts, allow me to suck you in, dear listener, allow me first to tell you the happy and glorious parts, so that you may become interested in our fates, and so that you may suffer along with me (again) when the story leads down those dark, rain-slicked alleys.

So I will begin at the beginning, or sufficiently close to the beginning to pique your interest. My name is Simon Pesco. I was born and raised in a pleasant, middle-class neighborhood in a pleasant Southern California city. Which one doesn't matter.

My father was a cop, and I decided early to follow in his footsteps. He was a member of the Technical Services Unit, otherwise known as the Bomb Squad. Yeah, Dad was a Bomb Technician until I was about fourteen years old. That was when one of the bombs happened and he lost two fingers and a big chunk of the palm on his left hand.

The only time that I ever heard my parents fight was after this incident.

One of his buddies had dropped Dad off at home from the hospital – he hadn't let Mom know what had occurred until he came home. He hadn't figured it was a life-threatening injury, so there hadn't been any need to worry her unnecessarily. At least, that's how he'd figured it.

When he walked into the house and told us what had happened, his hand was still a shapeless club of white bandages, and the idea that there were two less fingers in there grew up my little kid thoughts about my dad, raised him above hero status in my mind. But it was not so with my mom. She was pissed. At first I thought that she was only angry at him about how he'd handled breaking the news of his injury to her.

I don't know how the argument began, because I'm sure it began conversationally enough. I only started paying attention to their exchange when the shouting began. Mom began to cry, begging Dad not to return to the Unit. Dad shouted that it wasn't likely that they'd take him back with only eight fingers, now was it? To which my mom shouted that she knew they'd take him back if he asked, only eight fingers or not. She cried that it was too dangerous, that she didn't want her son to wake up one day to discover that he was an orphan. Dad yelled that the job wouldn't be quite so dangerous if he didn't have to work with incompetents. Mom yelled back that it was just like him to blame someone else – then she said quietly that if he didn't quit the Unit, she was leaving and taking me with her.

Dad was reassigned to a desk job in a different department not long after. Never did I hear him complain about the new position nor long to return to the Unit.

As I've said, I knew early that I wanted to follow in his footsteps. When I was a senior in high school, one night at the dinner table, I made some rebellious, ill-considered remark about maybe joining the Technical Services Unit myself, someday.

My mother replied mildly, "You most certainly will not," arose, and left the room.

I knew that there would be no further discussion, then or probably ever, about my becoming a Bomb Tech, lest I make my mother cry, and like sons everywhere, I didn't want to make my mother cry.

Irritated at her, irritated at myself, I dared to ask my dad, for the first time ever, if he'd really quit the Unit because she'd threatened to leave him.

Dad laughed. "She'd never said anything about the job before. She'd never let me know how much it bothered her – *before*. Hell, I'd always considered it safer than patrol – nobody ever took a shot at the Unit. But I found out that your mother'd worried, all those years, in silence.

"And when the accident happened – that's what we called it, Si," he'd lowered his voice, then. "We all called it *an accident*, but it was really Harrison's fault. The bikers had made a big stack of pipe bombs, and Harrison thought he's defused them all, but somehow he missed one." Dad shrugged. "Or maybe it was only half of one, but when I went in there to help him move out the rest of the explosives, somehow something detonated, something that should've been defused. Nothing but shoddy police work."

"So, they would've taken you back?" I asked.

Again Dad laughed. "Yeah. But some things are more important than a job, Si. Your mother said she didn't want to feel that I was in danger all the time. I wanted your mother to be happy. It was really a simple choice."

And when I graduated from high school, I didn't join the academy right away, because my mother wanted me to go to college first, to explore other options besides police work. Like my dad, I wanted my mother to be happy, but I was a little bit more hard-headed than him, I guess. I went to college, but I went for a degree in criminal justice so I could start off as a detective instead of a patrolman. As I knew it wouldn't be, the Technical Services Unit was not mentioned again.

But my dad never really forgot the Unit or the bombs. After the *accident*, he made bombs in the garage. He made bombs in the kitchen; in the basement; in the attic. Dad made bombs all over the house. No one would ever die, there'd never be any massive property destruction from any of my dad's bombs, however. Instead of exploding because of the dynamite or the C4 or the ammonium nitrate or the Detasheet, Dad's bombs would instead light up or make an annoying noise when they'd detonate, because there was nothing explosive in them. At most, there might occasionally be a little theatrical, harmless puff of smoke.

My dad built them, hid them, made mad bomber demands and penned ransom notes. I hunted them down and defused them. Then I reversed engineered them, made my own bombs, sometimes improved on his designs. Had him hunt for mine. I wasn't much on demands or ransom notes, however.

Through these somewhat unusual interactions did we remain a happy family. My mom loved the fact that her men remained close. Dad liked making bombs; I liked defusing them.

You might say that I was the All-American boy. My parents loved me and I knew it, and I loved them right back. I harbored no resentment about anything, never felt any kind of a desire to rebel, except for that one, ill-thought-out mention about joining the Unit. And that hadn't really been rebelliousness, as much as just a hurtful thing to say.

As a teen, I wasn't a goody-two-shoes, but somehow I never decided that getting drunk or stoned every day after school was the way to go. I was no athlete, but I was in the marching band.

I was never bored for long, because every couple of months I'd find an anonymous ransom demand tucked under my pillow, a threat stating that if I didn't come up with $30 million in non-sequential small bills by two pm the following Saturday, Mrs. Pesco was going to get blown to smithereens.

I didn't always find the bomb in time: sometimes the deadline passed without me locating the device. The game was real enough to me, and I felt all the adrenaline and fear during the search, and then the dejection if I failed. Although I knew that my mother wasn't really going to die, that there wasn't really going to be an explosion – the challenge remained.

One particular time, when the deadline passed and I hadn't been able to locate the device based on Dad's clues, I was frantic, just like I would've been, had there been a real danger. Mom worked in the office at the local high school, and I even broke down and called her, asked her to look and see if there was a bomb in her purse. It would be a little flashing device, a little plastic toy, something that didn't even resemble a fake bomb to anybody but us.

The goal would be to take it apart before the little red light went on, without *causing* the little red light to come on. The red light coming on would indicate that I'd failed, that I'd lost, that, had there been real explosives in the device, it would've detonated, killing untold innocent people.

My mom had sighed in annoyance, by I could hear the smile in her sigh. She told me to hold, checked her purse, and returned. "Negative, all clear here."

"Love you, Mom!" I told her, and went back to the search.

My dad was a very on-time bomber, and the deadline was long passed. Dad only made his mad bomber face at me – grinning, eyebrows raised, eyes wide – and was silent. It was very frustrating, but still I loved every minute of it.

It was only when Mom turned into the driveway after work that I saw the red light glowing behind the grill of her car.

"Dad blew up your car," I told her when she got out.

"Again?" she replied with a grin.

I gestured at the light, and opened the hood. I crawled around under the car and discovered that he'd rigged it to blow when the key was turned, a Mafioso cliché. I disconnected the fake bomb and reconnected my mother's ignition, and took the device inside.

"Too late," I said to Dad.

He held up his mangled left hand. "You can't win 'em all, son," he said and slapped me on the back.

It was a strange and maddening hobby, but the three of us loved it. I learned more about building and defusing explosive devices from this little game than I would've if I'd joined a hundred Technical Services Units.

Instead of being a Bomb Tech, I got assigned to Homicide, and I worked there for a few years.

Then all at once, Mom was gone. Complications after a "routine" thyroid operation, and she never woke up again. Three days after the funeral, Dad told me that he'd made some calls, pulled some strings. On Monday morning, I reported to his old Unit and began training. When I was through, I would be a Bomb Technician, just like I'd always wanted to be.

About two weeks before graduation from Tech School, I met Sandy while standing in line at the Starbucks down the street from the academy. Now, if I was the All-American boy, Sandy was the All-American girl, and then some. She was simply, irresistibly sexy in a fresh-faced, clean-scrubbed, girl-next-door-that-you-watched-through-binoculars kind of way.

What she saw in me, I'll never know.

When we spent our first weekend together at the beach, I knew that Sandy was the only girl for me. I'd found my other half.

From our first moments together, there on the cold sand, it was Sandy who decided on each new plateau in love-making. It was not as if she'd a set agenda, not as if she said, "No, we're not slated to try that yet." There was just an almost spiritual ebb and flow, a slow melding of tastes and desires, until at last, when it was time, I was surprised, yet not at all surprised. Far be it for me to sound like a feminist – wouldn't the boys at the station hoot, wouldn't they call me a pussy, and not at all under their breath – but sometimes I think that things might be better in this world if most men would just sit back and admit that some women should be allowed to decide when the correct time for action has arrived.

Whatever feminism I possess flies out the window, however, when I stress that it should only be *some* women who should be allowed to make these decisions. Some other women shouldn't be allowed to make any decisions at all. Some other women are just worthless from birth, as are some men. Some women don't deserve to draw another breath. I will eventually get around to telling you about at least one of them.

But I digress.

I was reminiscing about my beloved Sandy, and our first time together, that first weekend at the beach. What I learned from Sandy on that long weekend in the sand and surf was that women enjoy sex more than us. In the build-up to that single momentous squirt, we can never approach the peaks and valleys, the sighs and moans that they can encompass, if they're into it. And I think that's why most men hate them. When they're into it, we cannot possibly hope to achieve what they experience.

I guess if someone would've scratched me after that first weekend with Sandy, they *would've* found a feminist. I hadn't had an overwhelming amount of experience with women at the time, so I just naturally assumed that all of them were as knowing and as honest as Sandy, assumed that each of them was in the same perfect mysterious convergence with nature and her own body as she was.

Of course, I didn't verbalize these thoughts. I doubt if I even consciously recognized them. Sometimes, it's only through contrast and time, and other horrible events, that we can see another state of mind that we once embraced. We can only realize the person we were, sometimes, after we've become someone else.

On the trip home from the beach, I begged Sandy to marry me. She agreed, with one major condition. She'd marry me, but only if I went back to being a regular cop and gave up my nascent Bomb Squad ambitions. It was bad enough that I was a cop in the first place, she said, that I didn't seem to care that I might get shot. But a Bomb Tech? She said she could never spend the rest of her life with someone who was so cavalier about the imminent possibility of their own death.

I rebelled – maybe it was about time. Sandy and I didn't speak for the last week before my training ended. I graduated, made my dad proud, got drunk with him and his old pals. On Monday morning, I took my place in his old Unit as the rookie.

But I was completely miserable. When Dad asked me why I seemed so down, I told him about Sandy, about how she'd refused to marry me unless I gave up being what I'd wanted to be for so long.

Dad smiled, shrugged. "You have to make your woman happy, son, or you'll never be happy yourself," he told me.

Two weeks later, more calls were made, more strings pulled, and I transferred out of the Technical Services Unit, back to my old job in Homicide. On my way out the door, I couldn't help but overhear some of my dad's old friends from the Unit, and even some of the cops my own age, whispering a few words under their breath, such as *chicken,* and *yellow,* and even *gutless.*

Fuck 'em. I couldn't possibly have cared less about what any of them thought, because the week after that, Sandy and I got married.

Not long after we returned from our honeymoon, Sandy landed a job as a Park Ranger. I went back to being just a regular cop, just like my dad, protecting the commonwealth, apprehending the bad guys, looking out for the weak, upholding the right, et cetera. Any idealistic cliché you can think of, I embraced it.

To say I was naïve would've been the world's biggest understatement. But in my own defense, I must say that I was not unaware of my own naïveté. If I didn't know first-hand, I at least suspected that there were greater horrors and injustices in the world, major wrongs far beyond my small town detective's ability to right. But still, that was okay with me. I'd reconciled myself to the idea that, if I did the best I could, that couldn't help but make a difference. I believed my dad implicitly when he told me, whether it was about defusing bombs or solving murders, "You can't win 'em all."

So, I was joyous in my life. Work was rewarding, and I was the sincerest acolyte of my very own goddess cult, wherein, at her whim, I most sincerely worshipped my very own goddess. And I hoped it would continue, through careers and babies and life, until that time when I might peacefully lay down and die, old and successful, thanking the universe and my goddess for all the wonders I'd known.

I heard a saying once: if you want to hear God laugh, tell Him your plans.

I used to kid Sandy about her job, telling her that she wasn't a real Park Ranger – not like in a National Park. Her beat was the many not-too-wild and not-at-all-wooly little parks within the city limits of our little town. But she loved it, regardless – one park had a little concrete lined stream running through it, and another had a lake, and still another had a large enough pile of rocks to feature itself a "mount," if not a mountain. And all of these provided nature enough for her, and still kept her close to home and her cop husband.

Knowing now what I didn't know then, I can tell you that the beginning of the end started the night that Sandy and I witnessed the tiny meteorite crash into that very midtown "mount." We were sitting on the back porch, looking up at the sky. You can't detect too many stars in the city, but it was fun as always, just to be there in the cooling darkness with Sandy.

I spied a tiny dot of light streaking across the sky, and pointed it out to her. I'd like to tell you that it got bigger and bigger and nearer and nearer until we feared for our lives, just for the sake of suspense, but I'm too old and too tired to manufacture suspense so much at this point, and besides, it would be a lie. The thing looked like a tiny dot in the sky that suddenly just darted earthward, like a rogue firework on Independence Day.

But the odd phenomenon intrigued Sandy. "Let's go see if we can find it," she said with a grin. "Let's drive over to the park and see if there's a smoldering pile of ash and debris, like in the movies!"

"Park's closed after dark. Gate's locked," I said and yawned. "This cop's too tired to investigate." I smiled and reached over to hug her.

But Sandy leapt out of my arms. "We can still get in," she said, "because I know the Park Ranger. Come on, Si! Let's go!"

She dragged me by the hand out to her little roofless Park Ranger Jeep, and we drove the several blocks to the big hill that called itself a mount. It wasn't even a vaguely wild mount: a nice, paved one lane road snaked its way around and around, ending at a large paved parking lot at the summit. Halfway up, this road (called the *up road*) was crossed by a similar thoroughfare, which ended up on the other side of the hill; this was the *down road.*

I held a flashlight for Sandy while she undid the giant padlock that kept the gates secure at night, feeling all the while like the juvenile delinquent that I never was.

"I guess you'd have to say that this is a Ranger investigation," Sandy declared, and giggled like a little kid. "We'll drive up the road and if we don't find anything, we can snuggle for a minute under the trees at the top, look out at the city, like Lover's Lane."

The summit of the mount had served as Lover's Lane for many generations – many generations had no doubt been conceived there. But after a particularly gruesome accident involving a pick-up truck overcrowded with drunken kids, a roll over the side of the road, and a spectacular fire, the city fathers had at last closed the road to vehicular traffic. So any baby-making at the summit that occurred these days would only come after quite a little hike, and not a little trespassing, because the place was closed at night. So actually getting to drive up there was somewhat of a treat. Sometimes it pays to know the Park Ranger.

After unlocking the gate, I found myself slowly piloting the Jeep on the up road. Sandy turned on the spotlights attached to the Jeep's roll bar. She stood up and peered over the windshield into the darkness, searching for she knew not what. I just looked forward to *snuggling* at the summit.

But snuggling was not to be, as damned if we didn't locate the hellacious thing. It had clipped a street light – I told you that this was an urban park – whose bulb now hung loose and swung back and forth slowly, still illuminating, casting weird shadows, looking like an outtake from *War of the Worlds*. The meteor, now lit up by the Jeep's spots, had plowed up about three yards of the road's soft blacktop, and remained there, steaming.

It was like a cliché out of any and all alien invasion movies, and I cannot tell a lie, my friends and neighbors, I felt a little chill pass over me, looking at the thing. Here was something that was actually *extraterrestrial,* I thought, alarmed. It was truly not of this world. Who knew what outer space plagues it might carry?

I got out of the Jeep but didn't move very far away from it. While I was considering all these paranoid things, Sandy hadn't hesitated. Not hesitating was one of her guiding traits. She'd already leapt out of the Jeep and was unlatching the Jerry can full of water that was attached to the spare tire on the back. She succeeded in removing it, carrying it up to the meteorite, and was in the process of dumping water on it to cool it off – all before I snapped out of my *the Martians are coming* fugue.

The blacktop sizzled for a moment and then fell silent. Apparently it and the thing were sufficiently cooled then, as Sandy actually reached her hand into the little runway that it'd dug and touched it. Too late, I leapt into action, squealing, "Why are you touching it?"

She looked up at me, like I was an annoying pinhead. "Get the hammer and the shovel out of the back, will you?"

"The hammer and the . . .?" I said, confused.

Sandy arose and stalked past me, pressing my hand with the damp warmth from the thing, making me jump. She retrieved the aforementioned tools from the back of the Jeep and dug the lump of stone out of the road in less time than it takes to describe it, all while I just stood there stupidly.

Sandy put the tools back in the Jeep, and removed an orange highway cone. She walked back and put it over the hole in the road for the public works crew. Then she came back to me and held up her prize.

It seemed innocuous enough – nothing but a gray rock, the size and shape of a very large grapefruit or small Catawba melon. Sandy gestured for me to take it from her, but I shook my head. She called me a sissy.

"Maybe it's some kind of geode or something," she told me.

"A what?" I asked.

"How can you not know what a geode is?" I shrugged, and she plopped the rock onto the backseat. "I will explain, you dumb, uneducated cop, you." She flashed a smile at me.

We got back in the Jeep, Sandy driving now. She carefully turned around, then not carefully at all roared back down the up road. I held the flashlight again for her while she locked the big padlock.

I said, "You said you'd tell me what a geode is?"

"A geode is a hollow rock filled with crystals," she said. "They're beautiful."

"How do you know that's what it is?" I asked.

Sandy said, "I don't know if that's what it is. I'm just kinda hoping. It's pretty dull if it's just this gray rock."

I couldn't shake an utterly unfounded feeling of uneasiness. "How are you gonna find out if it's one of these geode things?"

Sandy grinned at me. "How do you think? I'm gonna bust it open."

But there'd be no interstellar geode opening that evening, because when we got back to the house, I was able to inveigle

Sandy into other activities. She mentioned something about getting a fresh start in the light of day with the thing, and set her prize on top of a small stack of magazines on a table in the living room. It sat there, forgotten, for the rest of the night.

When I arose the next morning, I walked right past the gray lump of rock, and almost made it out to the kitchen before turning around and giving it a second look. The thing had cracked in half during the night, you see, and seemed to have spread apart on its own, the way a person will crack open an egg and then spread the shell halves apart to allow the insides to plop out.

I peered at it. There were no sparkly crystals inside, as Sandy had hoped. Instead, there were six black-purple things, the color of an eggplant. They were ovoid shaped, about the size of small chicken eggs, stuck haphazardly inside the not-a-geode, four on one side and two on the other, in a similarly colored substance that reminded me of opaque Jell-O, or some kind of heavy equipment lubricant. As I watched, one of them inexplicably rolled out onto the cover of *Time Magazine* and came to rest over our president's eye, making him look like an eye-patched pirate.

I jumped, but didn't scream. I'm a cop, after all, and I seldom scream if I can help it. Instead, I called for my wife, still staring at the alien not-a-geode borne eggplant eggs. Studying the one that had rolled out, I noticed that it was not truly chicken-egg shaped. It was pointy like the Little Red Hen's product, but on both ends. The thing was pointy on both ends, instead of being rounded at the bottom like a chicken egg, and for some reason, this struck me as the most unnatural thing I'd ever seen. I shuddered even though I wasn't cold, and called for Sandy again.

She came downstairs yawning and scratching her head, totally oblivious to the *X-Files* style ominous-creatures-from-outer-space activity that was unfolding in her living room. Why was I the only one feeling this vibe?

Sandy approached and kissed me on the cheek. She asked me what I was yelling about. All I could do was nod speechlessly at the strange ambassadors from another world.

She glanced down at the eggplant-colored alien egg that had rolled out of the meteor. She smiled in delighted surprise, and said, "Will ya look at that!" Then before I could even flinch to stop her, she reached down and picked the thing up.

I made some incoherent choking sound in my throat and backed up a step. "Why do you always have to touch things?" I asked in exasperation.

"It's a rock, Simon." Sandy tapped it on the table.

I was thinking, *No, it's not a rock, it's something much more than that*, and that's when the growing certainty slithered into my mind. No. It wasn't a rock. *It was alive.*

But I couldn't actually say this out loud, because that's why they call them *irrational* fears. To say them out loud makes you look ridiculous.

"It's still a little warm," Sandy was saying, cupping the egg in her palm. Then she insisted on touching the meteor again. The not-a-geode; *the mother ship,* as I was beginning to think of it. "It must've cracked from cooling," Sandy opined.

She reached in and twisted another egg loose from its Jell-O. "What an odd formation," she said, and held the eggplant egg out to me.

I shook my head and backed away another step. I couldn't tell her that it didn't seem like any type of rock, any type of geological formation at all to me. Instead, I was convinced that it was some living thing, *an egg,* and its rock-like container was some kind of interplanetary shipping crate.

The next irrational thought that crossed my mind was that the shipment had been intentional, not just some random falling from the sky, but *a delivery*. If not, why hadn't it fallen somewhere else? In the ocean, in Siberia, in a forest somewhere where there was no one to hear it? Why did it choose to land in the middle of the city, if it wasn't meant to be immediately retrieved? I didn't feel irrational enough to believe that it was intended for us specifically, but it seemed as though there was *intention* nonetheless – the sender wanted someone to discover it as soon as possible.

Sandy held the egg-thing up to the light and turned it all around, as if it was one of those sparkly crystal things that she'd hoped for, instead of a completely opaque purple thing from Christ-only-knew where. She seemed mesmerized by it, as was I – except her attention was a charming child-like curiosity, whereas mine was a dread that I couldn't speak out loud.

Then suddenly, Sandy broke the spell, plopping the egg back into its sauce and looking at me. "I'll take it in and see what Hanson says." Hanson was her boss; he'd been a geologist before being called to the Park Ranger game.

I remember that Sandy's eyes were so blue that morning, her smile so full of love when she said, "Why do you look so frightened, Detective?" Then she hugged me and kissed me, and my groundless fears and imagined terrors of an extra-Earth invasion drained away. For several days, I thought no more of our maybe-dangerous visitors from outer space. Sandy had made the weird little things disappear, and few statements are truer than *out of sight, out of mind.*

Then, one morning, I reached across to steal Sandy's water glass from her bedside table – I always forgot to bring up one of my own – and bumped the interstellar not-a-geode which she'd placed there, almost knocking it to the floor. My hand brushed against it and it rattled, and when I looked over to see what it was that I'd touched, I couldn't jerk my hand back fast enough. My jerk was so violent, in fact, that it awakened my sleeping wife.

She yawned and eyed me with that beloved look of good-natured annoyance. "Why are you flopping around?" she asked.

All of my earlier, far-fetched, baseless fears had returned with a vengeance. Again I got the uncanny, ridiculous feeling that the thing was organic, not mineral. Now that I'd inadvertently touched it – something that I wouldn't have done willingly – the texture seemed to me as if it was made of some kind of hardened leather or snakeskin – some kind of grown or constructed thing, not a rock thing at all. A *container*, created by design.

"Why do you have that thing in here?" I answered her question with a question. My voice came out way too quavery, way too angry.

Sandy smiled. "I just think it's so cool." She sat up in bed and scooped the thing into her lap. She'd apparently discarded one half of the . . . *box,* I thought. She'd also washed off the gelatinous goop that had cushioned the eggs during their journey from the reaches of the universe. I shuddered to think of that alien purple-black slime sliding and congealing – or worse, dissolving and spreading – throughout the municipal sewer system.

"It's cool," Sandy repeated, still looking at the not-really-stone basket and the otherworldly eggs. "A one of a kind decoration, if you will," she said.

She picked up and caressed each ovoid shape, then gently replaced each back into its container. I noticed with renewed alarm that there were now only five eggs, and my imagination saw the missing one sprouting spiny legs and skittering away to commit mayhem, like that guy's head in *The Thing.*

Yeah. My imagination. A helluva thing is my imagination. Once upon a time, it was a joy and a comfort – I could always easily picture how things might've been in the oldie times or how they might someday be in the future times, and so on. It kept me entertained as an only child, did my imagination. Later, it helped solve crimes. I had a knack for picturing how the scene might've looked before the crime. I could picture how things had gone down, what was gone now that should've still been there, what was still there that should've been gone.

But after what happened to Sandy, my imagination became another enemy, showing me the blood and the screams and the fear and the pain, from all angles, coming up with new hypotheses on its own, over and over.

But they will all rue my imagination, will they not? Because without it, I never could've pictured where best to place the charges.

But I digress.

I looked at the five eggs nestled in their container, nestled in my wife's lap. "Where's the other one?" I asked.

She looked at me in surprise, then looked again into the bowl. It didn't take long to count to five, and she looked up at me again, confused.

"Did you give it to Hansen?" I asked.

"Hansen?" she asked back.

"Yeah. So he could tell us what it is?"

I watched Sandy count the five eggs again. "Yeah, I was going to do that, wasn't I? Yeah, I must've given it to him."

I was a little dismayed. "You don't remember?"

She looked at me again. I could see her consciously willing the confusion away. "Sure. I must've . . . I gave it to him the day after we found them," she said firmly.

"Has he figured out what they are yet?" I asked.

"He hasn't reported back to me yet," she said, a little mechanically, I thought. "With any, uh, findings." Sandy jumped out of bed, taking the extraterrestrial bowlful of alien eggs with her. "I know you don't like my moon rocks," she said, and walked out of the room. I heard the hall closet open and close, and then she returned. "There. Gonesville. No tiny green men will emerge and crawl into your ears while you sleep."

Sandy leapt upon the bed, and I quickly forgot all about the black-purple ovoids. I wouldn't think of them again for a long time and by then, well . . . A lot of people would be dead. *Gonesville.*

The next day, Sandy stayed in bed all day with the curse, as she insisted on so antiquatedly calling it. It was very bad for her every few months – she was forced to just lie in bed all day, curled fetally around a hot water bottle. She'd been trying new diets and new exercises to combat the pain, and things had

17

been improving. She'd not had any really bad ones for about six months.

But today, Aunt Flo had returned with the fury of a woman scorned. Over-the-counter remedies offered no relief, so Sandy took a pain killer and a sleeping pill and stayed in bed.

That was another good thing about Sandy – I guess it went really well with being a cop's wife and all – she wasn't much for pill popping. She said that pain medication made her feel as if her brain was wrapped in chenille. Soft and bumpy. So I knew that her cramps must be exceptionally bad this month for her to resort to taking a pain pill *and* a sleeping pill.

I made her favorite spaghetti dinner and brought it upstairs to her on a little tray. She opened her eyes and looked blankly at me for several seconds. I got the disturbing impression that she didn't recognize me at all.

After another heartbeat, she knew who I was again and gave me that beloved smile. She looked at the food tray and said, "I hope you brought that hysterectomy on the side."

I repeated her favorite line. "Hysterectomy? It damn near killed me." It was what she always said whenever she heard the word *hysterectomy.* I knew that if I didn't say it first, then she, without a doubt, would. It never got old. It was always funny to her.

"Seriously, Sandy," I said, watching her grimace in pain as she sat up. I set the tray cross her lap. "Maybe you should go see Dr. Kepler again."

"Dr. Kepler said I need to have a baby. She said that my cramps won't be so bad anymore, after I have a baby." Sandy glowered at me a little. "Now, you can either choose to believe that hypothesis or not – I'm not sure that I do. But either way, haven't we been trying to make a baby?"

I smiled at her.

"Then, am I not following my doctor's orders?" I nodded and she patted my hand. "I'm okay, Si."

I, who hadn't experienced any physical pain in my entire life, felt helpless in the face of Sandy's unknowable female troubles.

She flapped her hands in dismissal at the look on my face. "Seriously, Simon. I'm not gonna die. It's not any worse than it used to be. It'd just been getting so much better lately, that the same old cramps just seem worse." Again, she winced. "I'll be okay tomorrow. Next day at the most."

But she was not okay the next day. She wound up staying in bed for four whole days. I'd sometimes walk in there and find her staring blankly at the ceiling, and at these times it seemed like it would again take her a minute to recognize me. The little Park Ranger Jeep sat forlorn and dusty in the driveway.

I put in a call to Dr. Kepler, despite what Sandy had said about feeling better soon. The doctor finally returned my call and was in the middle of reassuring me that everything was probably okay, when Sandy at last emerged from our bedroom. She was fresh-scrubbed and glowing, her golden hair done up high in a cheerleader pony tail.

She told me, "Say, 'My wife seems to be all right now, Dr. Kepler.'"

I repeated the words into the phone, then handed it to Sandy. She had a little laugh with the doctor, then hung up. She looked at me again, and this time her annoyance seemed a little less good-natured than usual. She demanded, "Why did you call her?"

I told her that I was worried, and she reiterated that she'd told me that she'd be okay, and wasn't she now okay? I chalked up her snippy mood to that time, as any man would. I said again, "I was worried, babe. You've been in bed for four days."

She looked at me soberly, all anger fled. She hugged and kissed me. "Oh, Si! I love you so much! Promise that you'll never forget how much I loved you!"

Sometimes, people say things that just seem a little off, but we don't really examine the offness at the moment. It would only be later that I'd remember the weird phrasing, the odd fact that the tense was in the past. *Promise that you'll never forget how much I loved you!*

19

And by then – well, you know by now, gentle listener – by then, it would be too late.

Anyway, time grows short, and I wouldn't want to leave my story untold when the explosions start. So, I'll skip ahead in time and get to the important parts.

About a month later, Sandy brought home a new friend, someone that she said she'd met through work. Her name was Catarina Miner, but Sandy told me to call her *Catty*. She was the same age as Sandy, the same slender build. Except for the fact that Catty was a redhead and Sandy a blonde, they could've been sisters.

Now, the first time I met her, Catty looked at me with such frank appraisal that it bordered on the embarrassing. Sandy didn't seem to notice the way that her new friend ogled her old husband; but the woman's sly grins made me uncomfortable. She was just so out in the open about it.

Only a week after I'd met her, Catty even accosted me in our kitchen, grabbing me none too gently by the crotch and leaning in and biting my ear, telling me how much she wanted me – all that classic *Penthouse Forum* stuff. Not that I'm a ladies' man by any stretch, but just like they say in those somewhat predictable testimonials, this actually happened. I had to physically take her by the shoulders and gently but firmly push her away from me. I explained that while I was very flattered, blah, blah, blah, and while she was very attractive – which she was, and she knew she was – I loved my wife very much and would never do anything to jeopardize our happy life together.

Catty smiled nicely at me and took the rejection gracefully. She apologized for coming on too strongly, said Sandy was a lucky woman, smoothed out her clothing, and glided from the kitchen.

And that was the end of it.

I don't mean, "and that was the end of it," and she still winked at me, or patted me on the ass occasionally, or looked longingly at me. No, that was simply the end of it. Catty Miner never looked at me with that lustful appreciation again, because her lustful appreciation slowly transferred itself to someone else.

And that someone else was Sandy.

Now, I wouldn't want anyone to think that I have some deep-seated hatred of women, whatever their orientation. I know that'll seem like a feeble excuse after I murder as many of them as are unfortunate enough to be here when the timers run down – but believe it or not, I'm concerned with the idea that I may be misconstrued in my description of what happened next.

The best way that I can describe it is to have you imagine Sandy and Catty – beautiful, desirable, heterosexual women – imagine them standing back to back. Now imagine that each day, they turned a little to face each other, until eventually, they were locked in a passionate embrace. Like those giant clock works, where two figures roll out and strike a bell on the hour, then retreat back inside – that was Sandy and Catty. With each mechanical step, they moved away from me and toward each other.

Not long after I began to notice this, the others started showing up. In the end, there'd be six of them: Sandy and Cat (she wasn't *Catty,* anymore; she was someone else now) and their four butch friends.

I stood by in silence and watched as all these changes slowly occurred, with a sort of dumb amazement. Maybe I would've acted, or even *reacted,* if there'd been someone around to observe with me. If there'd been someone around to kid me, if there'd been gossip, if someone else would've seen and said, "God damn, Pesco, your wife has gone all lesbo on you! What the hell did you do to her?"

But there was no one.

Who could I discuss such a thing with? Not my fellow cops – there was not a lot of sensitivity going on there, on the best of days. Not my naïve, provincial father, in his basement, tinkering with bombs that never exploded. And I surely wasn't going to talk to any professionals. The shrink community can make all they want out of that statement after the fires go out,

21

but the truth be told, I didn't think that I needed any psychological help, as such. I wasn't sure what I needed. Mostly, I just felt a kind of speechless fascination.

And I missed the feel of Sandy's body intermingled with mine.

Because, as I've mentioned, I left the decisions of our sex life pretty much up to Sandy. As female animals in the wild do, she'd always clue me in through certain signals when she was amenable to entertaining me. They were fairly subtle sometimes, these signals – and every now and then I'd even been known to miss or misinterpret them.

But now those signals stopped. Not slowed. Stopped.

There were no arguments or guilty looks or recriminations from either of us. There wasn't even any discussion. It just gradually became as if we'd never been man and wife. There was love and affection, but nothing more than might've existed between a beloved brother and sister.

A different man would've spoken up. But I wasn't that man. I would not, *could not* whine and pule about suddenly being cut off from the Promised Land. Because, for better or worse – now there's an ironic turn of phrase – I loved Sandy with so much more than just my dick. And while I knew that she still so very much loved me, for some reason, she no longer wanted to love me with her body.

I was just going to have to wait and see how it all turned out.

So I just watched and wondered to myself. I smiled and hugged and kissed her goodbye when she took off to go out somewhere with Cat – who always seemed to look solemn and thoughtful and not at all like she was stealing my wife from me.

I must admit that I was mildly shocked and not only a little turned on when I quite by accident discovered the astoundingly graphic lesbian porn that they'd downloaded onto Sandy's computer. And it wasn't like we were having barbeques and luaus with the neighbors and there was whispering behind hands that my wife was turning into a dyke.

One by one, I was introduced to her new friends: there was Cat, of course, who now watched me as if I might be a spring, as if she believed that I was coiled with all kinds of masculine kinetic anger that could possibly be unleashed at any moment. And there was Chris, Pat, Taylor, and Billy, all the same age as Sandy and Cat and me, all in their mid-twenties, all appearing to have reached that age totally innocent of a man's touch.

If I was asked how I'd arrived at this opinion of them, I'm not sure that I could've put my finger on it. Somehow, I just knew – these were *lifelong* lesbians, not recent converts like Sandy and Cat. Maybe there was just something missing about them; maybe they just had something extra. I don't know how I knew. *I just knew.*

When I couldn't sleep some nights, usually after Sandy had hugged me and kissed me and snuggled up next to me, told me that she'd love me forever and then promptly fell asleep, I reflected on the idea that while Chris, Pat, Taylor and Billy had obviously always liked women, only Cat and Sandy had actually *turned,* going from *normal* girls to something else entirely, almost overnight. By rote, I repeat, not that there's anything wrong with that, until it happens to your wife, buddy – then you feel that there's something abnormal indeed going on. Not that Chris and Billy and Pat and Taylor weren't *normal* in their own circle, but my wife and the formerly quite heterosexual Cat had definitely been *turned.* Using a woman's prerogative, if you will, they'd entirely changed their minds. But why? Not so much how, though certainly – *how?* But most importantly, *why?*

I tried to blame myself, but that was just ridiculous.

I wondered with a wonder that I couldn't verbalize, how this had happened, why this had happened, how long it would it last, and what would become of my marriage by the time it was finished. I'd just about made up my mind to speak up, to say something, when Sandy announced that the six of them had decided to go camping for the upcoming three day weekend, a kind of prolonged girls' night out, and wasn't that just *wonderful?*

23

I helped them pack the sleeping bags and the Coleman stove into the back of Billy's Grand Cherokee; I reviewed with them how to start a fire. Again, Cat stood by solemnly while I kissed Sandy goodbye – I gave her a kiss on the cheek like a brother. Sandy again told me that she'd love me forever, gave me a hug, climbed into the back seat of the big Jeep. She and Cat waved goodbye, and the six of them were gone.

I kicked around the empty house by myself, sad, perhaps at last beginning to grow a little sullen. I reviewed their porn again, but it just didn't seem to have the same kick this time, seeing as how my gender was not represented, and similarly, seeing as how my gender – myself – no longer seemed attractive to my mate. I rehearsed things that I might say to Sandy when she returned – should I be hurt (which I was) or angry (which I was starting to become)? Should I ask, nay, *demand,* that my wife leave off interaction with her gay friends? How outrageously, ridiculously unfair would that be?

I heard the doors slam on the Grand Cherokee on Monday afternoon, and went out to help them unload the camping gear. I was met with *all five* women starting at me solemnly this time, not just Cat. It was kind of a shock, seeing them all standing there, just looking at me, eyes all round like orphans in a velvet painting. It was so weird that it caused me to stop and stare back at them.

That was when my wife came around the back of the Jeep, saw me, squealed in delight like a schoolgirl, and ran over and leapt into my arms. She covered my face with kisses.

"I missed you so much!" she cried, as if we'd been apart for months.

Sandy kissed me hard on the mouth, and I couldn't help but kiss her back, after all the days and nights of deprivation. Then I remembered our audience, and broke the kiss. Sandy opened her eyes and looked at me in surprise; I nodded at her friends, still standing there gawking.

How different her physically loving, wifely greeting at homecoming was from her sisterly farewell at leave-taking, I thought.

Sandy turned and addressed her posse, not bothering to get down from my arms. "Don't forget about all the fun new things we learned on our trip, ladies. Come over on Saturday, and we'll start our makeovers."

When they didn't move, Sandy shooed them with one hand, her other hand still holding onto my neck. The ladies at last complied and got back into the Jeep, without even bothering to unpack anything.

Except for Billy, who was driving, they all continued to stare at me with that same wide-eyed wonder as they drove away. All except for Cat, that is, whose gaze seemed to've curdled a bit at Sandy's exuberant display of affection for me. Cat's expression bordered on one of those *if looks could kill* kind of things. For some reason, this brought a smile to my face, and I gleefully nodded goodbye to her. She looked away.

When they were gone, I was left standing in the driveway with my wife in my arms, like a new bridegroom. Sandy whispered in my ear, "I feel so musty from the woods. Would you like to take a shower with me?" And then she giggled.

I was so dumbfounded, so entranced by that giggle, that I would've followed her off a cliff like a lemming, had she but crooked her little finger and bade me join her. There was a sexy sparkle in her eyes, just for me, just like in the old days, and I dared to hope that perhaps, somehow, some way, I'd gotten my old Sandy back.

She practically dragged me toward the shower, dropping her clothing and pulling off and dropping mine as we went. I followed along silently, grinning like an idiot schoolboy, afraid to speak and break the spell. Eventually we made it into the shower, where Sandy turned on the water and lathered me up as if I was the one who'd been in the woods for three days, doing God-only-knows what with five (other?) lesbians.

Sandy gave me what would've been a slow and languorous hand job, had not my utter surprise and recent celibacy been issues. Instead, it was pretty quick indeed, as if I really was that idiot schoolboy. Then she rinsed me off and playfully pushed me out of the shower, telling me that I should go get into bed now and wait for her to finish scraping the camping dirt off. I simply nodded, still not daring to speak.

As I slid in between the crisp sheets, impatiently waiting for my beautiful wife to join me for a little marital activity, I wondered if perhaps I could've somehow imagined the weirdness of the past epoch. After all, I'd never actually *witnessed* any hanky-panky between Sandy and Cat. Or between any of the other ladies either, for that matter. No public displays of affection – I couldn't tell you who was with whom or anything like that.

As I waited in bed, I tried to try to talk myself into the idea that I'd simply imagined that the other ladies were gay, and that my wife and her new best friend had seemed to turn gay, also. Then I realized that it would be ludicrous to make this attempt. My observations were just that. I hadn't imagined any of it.

The things we can talk ourselves into. The things we can rationalize. The things we can ignore.

But then Sandy was there with me for the first time in what seemed like forever, and I wasn't talking myself into anything, wasn't rationalizing anything, wasn't ignoring anything. I was just reveling in the familiar smell and taste of her, something that I'd so missed, so longed for. It was absolutely wonderful – she was my same old Sandy again, but she was also like a new and different woman. I figured that perhaps a little absence did make the heart, as well as other parts, grow fonder.

Afterward, we laughed and talked and snuggled, just as we always had before, and it was as if the intervening "gay days" had never occurred. I certainly wasn't going to bring them up. It was one of the most pleasant afternoons we'd ever spent together.

All that week, Sandy couldn't seem to get enough of me. It was like we were newlyweds again.

Then on Saturday, the world got a little strange again. At about ten am, Sandy and I were interrupted during another re-enactment of our wedding night when Billy, Taylor, Pat, Chris, and a somewhat self-conscious-seeming Cat showed up at our house en masse. They carried shopping bags and makeup cases and clothes on hangers, and immediately began a massive make-up and hair-doing session that rivaled the local cheerleader's house on Prom Night.

Now it was my turn to stare, open-mouthed, at them.

There was hair-cutting and hair-dyeing, and powders and foundations and perfumes. There were sexy bras and fishnets and short skirts and barrettes and something that looked like an Inquisition torture device. When I pointed at it in alarm, Sandy laughed and told me it was an eyelash curler. I was not even aware that eyelashes could be or ever needed to be curled. There were eye shadows in blues and greens and tans and browns, sparkly and glittery. There were lipsticks in pinks and reds and crimsons. There were shrieks and laughter and oohs and ahhs.

Throughout the process, they all traipsed through the house immodestly, half dressed, ignoring me completely, as if I was the harem eunuch or the stage manager at the strip club.

Then suddenly they were finished and the ladies were transformed. Mousey Pat had become a stunning redhead, somewhat more sophisticated-looking than natural-redhead Cat. They dressed up chubby Taylor so that she no longer seemed overwhelmed by baby fat – now she was zaftig, voluptuous. Magical makeup softened the hard, bull-dyke edge to Billy's mouth, and a radical hair-cut made Chris cease entirely to appear to be someone's sensible-shoes wearing, hippie cousin. A little eye shadow and dark lipstick returned Cat once again to the sultry beauty I remembered. Sandy didn't need any makeup to be beautiful to me – she was always beautiful to me, and her recent return to the ranks of the heterosexual was all that was necessary to restore her to the charming young woman that I loved so much.

Because I was the only male present, the task of perusing and passing judgment on the ladies' new looks fell to me. *How utterly bizarre* - the thought insinuated itself into my brain –

27

how completely bizarre, that suddenly they want a man's *opinion.*

Sandy sat me down in the living room and paraded them by me, one by one. She asked me pointed, personal, entirely inappropriate questions about them: do Chris's boobs look too small? Should Pat wear her new hair up or down? How does Billy's ass look in this skirt? It was as if Sandy didn't care that they were standing right there.

Billy, Taylor, Pat, and Chris all smiled like happy little girls playing dress-up – they didn't mind Sandy's cattle-call comments and questions to me, and they each looked sheepishly at me, unable to disguise that they were each very anxious to hear my opinion. This was obviously some kind of first-time experience for them. Of course, I pronounced them each and all lovely, and tried to forget that I'd somehow stumbled into *The Twilight Zone.*

But what was the motivation to abruptly become so girly?

Before I could consider *that* idea for too long, Cat slinked by, all woman, and favored me with that same smoldering glance that she used to apply, once upon a time. For a change, she hardly looked at my wife at all.

Just what the hell was going on here?

After the makeshift catwalk festivities were over, all that feminine pulchritude giggled and flounced out to the kitchen and made lunch. I felt as though I was the guest of honor, like they were treating me for some reason. As if, what I couldn't help but think of as the *new* girls – Billy, Taylor, Pat, and Chris – were somehow trying to impress a man for the first time. First with their new femininity, and if that wasn't sufficient, then with their cooking skills. I must say that they did well. They made me feel like a king – but on the other hand, I was the only king present. A lesser man might've believed he deserved it all anyway, just because he was the only man there. To me, it was just another odd afternoon in a life that had become one odd afternoon after another.

At one point, while we were all gathered around the table eating, the laughter and conversation suddenly died away, and once again, I found them all staring at me. That is, all the *new* girls were staring at me. After a heartbeat of complete silence, Sandy and Cat tried to revive the conversation, but it was dead at the scene. Billy, Taylor, Pat, and Chris would simply not join back in. They just stared at me like I had two heads – as if I was something so out of the ordinary that they couldn't help themselves.

After some uncomfortable seconds of this, Sandy startled us all by clapping her hands together like a headmistress. "Come, come, ladies!" They all looked at her like obedient pupils, except for Cat, who'd now decided that *she* was going to stare at me for a while.

"I think we're finished here, are we not?" Sandy asked. "Let's go look at those places we picked out."

I asked her what places, and before she could reply, Cat answered automatically, "Billy is looking for a new apartment. She asked us to help her out. We have a list of places to go look at today."

The ladies had all turned to look at me again when I spoke, with the same blank curiosity that they may have afforded a talking dog. So Sandy clapped her hands again, and as one, they turned and looked at her. I was uncannily reminded of the other-worldly blonde children from *The Village of the Damned*.

"Shall we go, ladies?" Sandy asked, and they nodded and mumbled and slowly filed out, leaving behind half-eaten sandwiches, clotting soup. Sandy smiled at me and said, "Since we were so nice to fete you, would you mind cleaning this mess up?"

I told her that I wouldn't mind at all.

Out of nowhere, Sandy suddenly kissed me passionately, right there in the kitchen.

"I love you," she whispered breathily.

I told her that I loved her, too, and when she turned to go, I followed her out. I was just curious enough to walk out there to see if they'd all stare at me again. They did and it was not any less creepy for being expected.

When they pulled out, I waved, and all the new girls waved in unison. Cat decided to ignore me this time. Sandy blew me a kiss.

Weirdness begets more weirdness, or so it seemed in my life at the time. Curiouser and curiouser. For the next week or so, I was treated every night to my beautiful wife in a different sexy lingerie get-up. It was sort of a racier, Sandy-only version of the previous *Twilight Zone* fashion show, and Sandy followed it up every night with more fantastic sex. She was wild and seductive: pretty in pink, devastating in blue, ferocious in red, demure in white, tantalizing in black.

Somehow, I got the impression that she was rehearsing for something. What it could've been, I couldn't've imagined at the time. I might even have become a little jealous at this idea, had I not known that I was the only guy for Sandy. The thought that there might be another man, that she might be auditioning all these teddies for me in preparation for showing them to *him,* didn't enter my mind. I was the only guy for Sandy – she was not the cheating type. I knew her.

In the two weeks before I got the call, I never saw the new girls again. It was as if they'd simply disappeared back to whence they'd come. And I only saw Cat a couple of times. That old devouring look was back in her eye – but I got the unpleasant feeling that she didn't want to fuck me anymore. Now she actually wanted to *eat me.* Like with a knife and fork.

But enough of this introduction. Time to spill the beans. Time to tell you what happened to Sandy. Time to tell you what happened to my wife and try to offer up some explanation as to why I'm gonna blow up a lot of seemingly innocent people.

The last time I talked to my wife was on a Friday morning, right before I left for work. She informed me that she and all her friends would be spending the weekend at Billy's new apartment, decorating and rearranging furniture and unpacking and all those fun things. She didn't ask me if I wanted to help, didn't invite me to come along. She simply reminded me that she'd love me forever, gave me a sweet kiss, and watched me walk out the door.

Cat called me at about two in the morning, Saturday night. I guess that would officially be called Sunday morning.

"Si, honey," she whispered, "if you'd like to know what your little wife is really doing at Billy's *apartment,* the address is," and she slowly enunciated the numbers and the street name. It was in the next town over, a little bit larger municipality, a little bit rougher than our little burg.

Still half asleep, I asked her what the hell she was talking about. She giggled nastily and said, "We've scheduled quite the little party, you see, me and the girls. And of course, your loving Sandy. And the men. Can't forget them, now can we? Without them, it wouldn't be much of a party at all."

Again, I asked her what the hell she was talking about. Again, she giggled. "It's been nice knowing you, Si – although I always did think you were a little bit of a pussy for not taking me up on my original offer. Are you awake now? Let me give you that address again." And she recited the number and the street again and hung up.

Yeah, I was awake now. It was just strange enough, just scary enough, that I got up and got dressed. I headed in the direction of the address she'd given me. I was familiar enough with the next town over and where the street was, even though I'd never really driven on it, just passed by the exit to it. It was about a forty minute drive away.

When I took the exit, I noticed a pay phone on the street corner, in front of a boarded-up 7-11. Now there's something that you hardly see any more at all, nowadays: a pay phone. But back then, they used to be everywhere.

Call it cop's intuition, call it husbandly fear, call I whatever you like. But I felt that there might really be something wrong, and if there was, I'd like some back-up. I was also just unsure enough – maybe Cat was drunk or something? – that I didn't want to call the local PD and identify myself, just in case nothing was actually amiss. In case this was some kind of nutty joke or something. So I dialed 911 on the payphone, muffled my voice, and called in a domestic disturbance complaint for the address that Cat had given me. And before I hung up, just in case, I wiped off any fingerprints. I thought that there probably weren't any cameras around, because the 7-11 was boarded-up; if there were, I couldn't do anything about it anyway, and I'd worry about all that later, if there was any worrying to be done.

I arrived at the scene about another half an hour later. Some cop I was. I'd driven by the place twice – I'd missed it because I'd been looking for an apartment building. There were no apartments anywhere; it was some kind of warehouse district. Anyway, when I finally found it, the place was already crawling with cops, just like on *CSI*. Cruisers, ambulances, a fire truck, the whole nine yards.

I figured that maybe I hadn't been the only one that'd made a noise call.

You know how, in the movies, the worried, frightened spouse always runs up to the police line and gets held back? Then the patrol cop calls some Bassett Hound-eyed detective, who comes over and reluctantly, sadly, tells the distraught spouse the bad news?

Yeah, well, all that wasn't going to happen to me. If my wife was in there, then I was going to get in there, and not after any police red tape. So I hung my shield on its chain, and also like you see in the movies, I waved it at the patrolman, and he lifted the tape and let me pass.

Contrary to television, all cops at a crime scene don't know each other. We can find out anything we want about each other with just a few phone calls, if the need strikes us, but we all don't automatically know each other at a crime scene.

The place was a converted warehouse of some sort. I never did find out what it'd been before it became what it became. Double doors led inside to a staircase. I heard Cat whisper *quite the little party* in my head. Apparently whatever that had been was upstairs.

The walls of the stairwell and the stairs themselves were heavily tagged; so much so that it smelled like old spray paint in there. The stairway was lit by a few bulbs in shades shielded by heavy wire mesh. I just walked calmly up with the ebb and flow of police personnel, all our footsteps echoing dully off of the diamond-plated aluminum of the steps.

The top floor was ablaze with light from overhead fluorescents. Whatever it had once been in its warehouse days, I couldn't tell you – it was just a large, oblong room. It now housed six bays, their partitions attached to the back wall, with an open hall passing between the other end of the partitions and the opposite wall. It reminded me of a hospital emergency room. The partitions separating the bays were thin, just drywall partitions, not reaching to the ceiling. There were curtains for privacy attached to the ends of each bay. Every one of them had been pulled back – the cops were here; there was no more privacy.

There was a bed in each bay. Just like in the ER, the beds were adjustable, and each had a set of gleaming metal stirrups attached. Like sometimes in the ER, each bay except for one contained two people.

And just like in the ER, there was lots and lots of blood.

I stepped in behind the police photographer for a closer look. In the first bay, his flash made Pat's creamy skin and faux-red hair, kohled eyes and orange-tinged lipstick seem a little garish. The fact that she was wearing only a yellow tube top, black pumps, and black lace ankle socks didn't help toward a lady-like appearance. Nor did the fact that her bed was propped up, and her feet were in the afore-mentioned stirrups. Pat stared straight ahead.

From directly below her brand-new belly button ring, someone had ripped her open, as if with Freddy Krueger knives. This had happened so recently that blood still oozed from the wounds.

Pat was dead, as was the muscular young Hispanic man lying on his back on the floor of the bay. He wore an expression of surprise; Pat's blood dripped onto his forehead. He was nude; someone had apparently surgically removed his genitals. Of his blood, there seemed surprisingly little.

Leaving the photographer to finish his thankless task, I moved on to the next bay, slowly, calmly. No need to draw attention to myself. I'd always been such a good cop, and I blended in with this force, going about their investigative duties, speaking in subdued voices, quickly and efficiently doing their jobs.

In the next bed was Billy. She was naked, save for black fish nets clotted with gore. The garter belt and garters that'd been attached to them were gone, no doubt ripped away by the same knife that had butchered her abdomen. Billy's partner – they were so obviously couples – was a tall black kid, maybe all of twenty. He wore only basketball shoes and socks, soaked with Billy's blood. His genitals had also been cut away.

Still I walked slowly, surveying the carnage in each bay. Each one of Sandy's friends, dressed as a whore, dead, gutted, accompanied by some equally dead, equally mutilated dude.

Next was Chris. Her bed wasn't propped up, but her bare feet were in the stirrups. Her face was turned to one side, and viewed over her bloody knees, I could only tell it was her because I recognized the new haircut.

A redheaded guy lay on the floor beside her, his skin the color of milk. Insanely, I noted that the rug indeed matched the drapes – the hair on his chest was exactly the same shade as the hair on his head. I imagined that his pubes would've been the same color, had there been any pubes left to inspect. They had gone with his genitals.

Next was chubby Taylor and an equally chubby young man, apparently of Middle Eastern descent. His arms and chest were covered with very good tattoos. Both dead, both mutilated.

I was running out of Sandy's friends, but still I didn't hesitate. I moved on to the second to last bay. By this time, it didn't take a cop's intuition to know that it would be either Cat or Sandy. And since Cat had called me, almost as if she'd wanted me to find all of this, I was pretty sure that I wasn't going to find her here, eviscerated like a deer.

And, of course, gentle listener, the woman in the next bed was Sandy. She was lying flat on her back, her legs not in the stirrups, but hanging over the end of the bed. She was wearing some kind of nurse's uniform, costume-like. The white stockings and white high heels were flecked with chunks of tissue and blood. Cold flames of scarlet snaked up the cheap nylon. Mercifully, the uniform was pulled down over her abdomen. It appeared as though she'd been stabbed right through her clothes, so the material mostly covered the wounds to her stomach. An old-fashioned nurse's hat had fallen forward and obscured her face. But there was no mistaking it; the dead body in the second to last bay was my wife, my love. My other half.

In my mind I heard her say, *Promise me you'll always remember how much I loved you!*

I looked over beside the bed. I couldn't see Sandy's partner's face, because he was lying on his stomach – thank God for small favors, I guess. All I could see was a nice tan and a shock of very blonde hair. He had a tattoo of the Earth with a knife through it on his ass.

There was another bay and another bed – *Cat's place*, I thought. But it was empty of bodies, quick or dead, just like I somehow knew it would be. There was just a tiny spray of blood on the sheets at the end of the bed, between the stirrups.

I heard a technician in the room to my left whisper, "The women, they were all stabbed repeatedly. But these guys – the cleanest wounds I've ever seen! Like surgery!"

His partner said solemnly, "Just like cattle mutilations. Very little blood."

So how should I explain what happened next? I just stood there, gazing at my dead, mutilated wife; her dead, mutilated friends; five dead, mutilated dudes. But to say that I even gaped would be stretching it. I'd never seen a sex-mutilation multiple murder quite like this one – but I'd seen quite a few murder scenes. I was a Homicide Detective, after all. I'd also seen a few very bloody suicides, and some astonishingly gruesome car wrecks.

So, no, I didn't gape, or rave, or cry, or anything like that. I just stood there. Looking. You could say that it might've sprung from my ambivalence toward the possibility of a higher being, spiritual redemption, or an afterlife – or maybe you could attribute it to the fact that I am a professional, with my emotions in check. Or perhaps, I was just numb with shock.

But regardless, dead is dead, people. Sandy was just meat, now – whatever made her Sandy, whatever made her who I loved, was gone. And becoming hysterical and catching her ruined corpse up in my arms like some piteous Romeo would not, as they say, bring her back. And it would've gotten me handcuffed and hustled right into the back of a patrol car, before I could find out anything about what had occurred here.

Still, it was true that I was in shock. Some rational part of my mind told me that the grief and outrage would come later. The pain, too, my mind assured me – the merciful numbness that now enveloped me would wear off, leaving behind a gaping hole in my soul that would feel just like those gaping holes in Sandy and her friends.

But for the moment, I just stood there, looking. Over and over again, I thought, *why did this happen?* And, *where is Cat?* The questions in my head varied a little – sometimes it was, *how did this happen?* And, *why isn't Cat in there dead with them?*

I knew that all my questions would be answered if I could only find Cat. I already knew the where and approximately the when. Cat would know the who, the how, and most importantly, the *why*.

As I say, I didn't gape, but my lack of motion in the busy hive of impersonal crime scene techs eventually attracted attention. I was not dramatically pointed out as an interloper, nor tackled and dragged from the room, or anything like you see on TV. One of the detectives simply sauntered up and stood next to me, surveying the scene in the same manner that I was.

At last he spoke. "Helluva thing, huh?"

I turned away from the carnage and met his eyes. His expression seemed to be one of mild curiosity, but I could see a

36

cop's hard resolve nested beneath. I knew that while he seemed mild now, if I made any move to walk out of there – if I made any move at all – I'd be restrained quicker than it takes to say it. But there was a certain kindness in those eyes, too.

He glanced at my badge on its chain and said, still with that mildness, "I see that you're with our neighbors to the south. You're a bit out of your jurisdiction, aren't you?"

I felt that if I was ever going to get to the bottom of this, I was going to have to trust someone, and I felt that my best choice would be this guy. I leaned in so no one else could hear me, and told him softly, "I'd like to talk to you outside."

He whispered back, "And why is that?"

I nodded at the nearest bed. "The one in the nurse's get up? That's my wife."

The surprise registered in his eyes, but before he could speak, there was a general shout and jumble of noise, voices, doors being kicked open. All eyes turned toward a large supply closet to the right of the bays, which had apparently gone unexamined, uninvestigated, until just that instant. One of the uniforms, bored with all the blood and guts, had thought to himself, "Gee, I wonder what's in here?" and had opened the door, had switched on the light.

Sometimes the embarrassment of shoddy police work is not to be believed. It was both refreshing and disconcerting to see that it didn't occur in just my jurisdiction.

And embarrassment was no doubt exactly what the uniform felt when he flicked that light switch. He'd probably been expecting to find nothing but a bunch of brooms and mops. Instead, he'd found a naked skinhead sitting on the floor against the wall in the corner.

The only thing that saved the poor guy from getting shot, I would think in retrospect, was that the uniform was too utterly surprised to just instinctively pull his weapon and fire. By the time he got his gun out, it had registered in the uniform's mind that the skinhead wasn't a threat, because he'd already assumed the position – hands laced behind his head, head down on his knees.

Still, there was a lot of shouting and scuffling, cursing and door-kicking, as they dragged the guy out and cuffed him. The detective I'd been talking to told me, "You don't leave," and turned to where they'd hauled the guy to his feet and brought him out. I blended in with the crime scene techs, who'd now formed a circle around the guy, the detective, and the two other cops that were holding him. I stood on tiptoe, looking over someone's shoulder, to see just what it was that the uniform had discovered.

The guy was a little younger than me, no more than twenty-five, maybe; although the fear in his eyes made him seem much younger. The fear was at odds with the rest of him: old scars from what appeared to be the losing side of a knife fight crisscrossed gang and prison tattoos on his arms and chest and belly. This kid was no creampuff – it was obviously not the swarming cops that he was afraid of.

I watched him search the faces of those gathered around him, until he found the man in charge, my detective buddy, who was standing right in front of him. Then he began to rant. "It was robots, man! Chicks with lasers and helmets like Darth Vader, but with tentacles!

"I heard Rusty scream, and I started to back up to go see what was wrong. But Kitty – yeah, she said her name was Kitty – she tried to pull me back to her, and then I felt some kind of a tug on my nuts. I looked down – she wasn't human, man! There was this . . . this *thing*, this metal *thing* coming out of her, and it almost had me, and she was saying, 'Oh, Sammy, come back, I want you!'

"But there was this metal thing, and I jumped back and socked her in the mouth. I backed out of the booth and Rusty was screaming, and there were all these other chicks down there by his booth. They had on latex cat suits, and weird Darth Vader looking helmets, and they had tentacles, like a fucking octopus. And they had some kind of laser guns in their hands – one of them went into Rusty's booth and he stopped screaming, and I heard his body hit the floor. So I grabbed my gat and hid in that closet over there."

Bewildered, someone said, "Gat?"

The skinhead looked smug. "Yeah, man. There's a gun in there. It's under a box of toilet paper, right by where I was sitting. I never go anywhere without my pistol." He grinned and I noticed he was missing both front teeth. "I coulda had the jump on all of you."

There was more scuffling and muffled shouts while someone recovered the pistol.

The skinhead continued. "I was gonna blow any of them chicks away if they tried to come in there and get me. But after they shot Rusty with their laser guns, I guess they shot everybody else, too, 'cause I heard a lot of bodies hitting the floor. Then I heard Kitty crying and pleading – I could hear her voice, but I couldn't make out what exactly she was saying.

"Then there was some whirring noises – it was so fucking weird! I stayed in there. I was gonna stay in there forever. What else was I supposed to do? There was at least three of them, and they had those ray guns, and I was naked . . ."

The skinhead glanced down at his nakedness, and now he started to scream, "Oh, my God!" over and over again. He was looking down at himself and screaming, so the nearest uniform looked in the same direction, and I watched him cover his mouth with his hand like a woman and look away.

"My dick!" the skinhead screamed. "Oh, my God, *she cut off my dick!*"

Now I wasn't the only one standing on tiptoe to see what we could see. The detective peered down at the organ and said, "I'm not gonna touch it, Sammy, even if I am wearing gloves. But I've got good news for you. She didn't cut it all off."

He nodded at someone, and they took naked, handcuffed, partially castrated Sammy away. He still raved about robots and chicks with laser guns, but mostly he screamed about the loss of his member. He didn't even seem to notice the gutted women and castrated men in the bays. Maybe he didn't look on purpose.

The techs went back to their work, shaking their heads. The detective came back over to me. His manner held no suspicion of me now, if it ever had. He peeled off the latex gloves he was wearing and offered his hand. "I'm Solomon Nova. Call me Solly."

I shook his hand and introduced myself, and he asked if I still wanted to go outside. I nodded. To make a long story short – the timers might not actually be ticking, but they're still counting down – we sat in his car and I told him what I knew. He didn't write down what I said like a cop, but simply listened like a friend.

And eventually we became friends, and eventually I transferred to his jurisdiction and we became partners.

It didn't take long for me to discover that Sol was what you'd call a *ladies' man.* He was classically good-looking – the only reason that he wasn't a movie star, I guess, was that he'd never wanted to be a movie star. He had coal black hair and light blue eyes, and what I've heard described as a killer smile.

But don't take my word for it – I've never been much good at describing the attractiveness of other men. Here's an example for you – we were in a bar once, Solly and I, and as we passed by, I heard a young woman say to her friend, "He's so *fine*, it *hurts* to look at him." And I knew she wasn't talking about me.

I don't recall if Sol wound up taking that particular woman home – but if he'd wanted to, I'm sure he did. Even though I mixed up every tense possible in that sentence, it sums up Sol Nova completely. Any woman he'd ever wanted, he got, without effort. This was so true that, through my association with him, I had to reimagine what *want* and *get* really meant.

When it came to our opinions of women, to say that Sol and I were polar opposites would be an understatement. I told him how wonderful Sandy had been, I told him how she'd always been like a goddess to me. He never questioned my opinion of her, even though I knew he must've wondered how I could still think of her as a goddess after the way she'd ended up.

But if I never succeeded in showing him how women could be goddesses, Solly did succeed in showing me, nearly every day, how they could be nothing but tools. And to be fair, before you judge Solly too harshly, it was really the girls that proved *themselves* to be tools.

Allow me to elaborate. Remember how I said that Solly, with those movie star good looks, could have any women he wanted? Well, it could be said that he'd never had to want for them, really, not ever. For earliest childhood, or so he told me, he'd just have to bat those baby blues at teachers, babysitters, shop girls – and he got an extra pat on the head, or to stay up late, or a free candy bar.

And from about fifteen on, he got that other thing, too, and just as effortlessly.

I lost several hundred dollars to him, before I refused to bet anymore, on this wager – Solly would say, "We can walk into any establishment – bar, restaurant, store, funeral home, church – and you, Simon, my friend, you point out any woman – and I will get her phone number."

"*Any* woman?" the sucker asks. "Anywhere?"

"Yep," Solly would reply. And he wouldn't even smile.

He never lost that bet. And as our friendship wore on, he'd listen attentively when I'd tell him how perfect and incredible Sandy had been. And when the opportunity presented itself, Solly would demonstrate to me how the rest of her gender would always do whatever he asked. Every time.

If you're expecting to next hear about how some great romance overtook Solly, about how he finally met the girl that turned him down, and thereby decided he was in love, and how he knew he had to win her through his heart and not his looks, and so on – you're looking in the wrong place. It never happened.

Unlike a lot of guys I know, Solly didn't hate women; he didn't even dislike them. They were just tools to him, as I've said. But before you judge him or write him off as a bad guy, I must point out that he appreciated their beauty and their intelligence and whatever else a person appreciates in the opposite sex. But that was as far as it went. There was absolutely nothing mysterious or at all awesome about them to

him. Every woman was just like a good waitress to Sol –
smiling, friendly, there exactly at the right moment when you
need your ice tea refilled. But he cared no more deeply for any
of them than you do for that efficient waitress.

Sol had learned from his high chair that if he threw a toy
on the floor, his mom or his sister would pick it up for him; if
he asked for an extra cookie, the sitter would give it to him; if
he wanted to sit in the front of the class or in the back, all he
had to do was ask the teacher. And if he walked into a bar and
smiled at that redhead, she'd smile back, and everything else
would proceed along familiar lines toward the inevitable
conclusion he desired. It was like the sun rising to him. All he
had to do was ask.

We were both twenty-six when we first met, and I once
asked him how many women he thought he'd slept with.

He looked at me in surprise. "I have absolutely no idea,"
he said. I supposed he began to tote them up then, because after
a pause, the very next thing he said was, "Si, you embarrass
me!"

But while Solly himself claimed that he didn't know how
many, I imagined that they were legion. He'd wax
philosophical on all the different types of women to me
sometimes; *goddess* was never one of his categories. He'd tell
me cautionary tales about which types to avoid. Mostly I
listened to him, because I figured he knew what he was talking
about.

But every now and then, he'd come up with some wild,
off-the-wall story, and I'd tell him he was full of shit. Then
without hesitation, he'd pull over at the nearest bar, drag me
inside, pick up some unsuspecting woman (or more correctly,
allow *her* to pick *him* up), and then amaze me all over again by
predicting exactly what she'd say or do next. He was
astounding.

But other than using this – for lack of a better word, *skill* –
to sometimes relieve me of twenty bucks when he was a little
short, Solly didn't brag about it. It was old news to him. It was

just the state of the world: women were there to be had. Period. Next problem.

Solly and I never did solve the massacre in the warehouse, not in the whole eighteen years since we started working together, since it happened. Not until just this week, and then, well, I pretty much had it solved for me.

No one is going to believe a word of it, of course.

Just like no one is going to believe that this bastion of upright femininity is – or was, once I blow it to smithereens – that it was, in reality, a nest of some of the most fantastic and unbelievable mass murders ever known to mankind.

But I digress.

After I met and befriended Solly, my transfer over to his jurisdiction was a straight shot. Everyone in my own precinct was sad to see me go, but they all understood why I had to leave. No one ever had the nerve to say anything to me about the circumstances in which Sandy had died. But they all knew about it, and the facts of it made some of them too uncomfortable to be in the same room with me. Some of them just couldn't fathom how I could show my face, how I could go on being a cop, when my wife had died just like one of the whores executed by Jack the Ripper. Some of them no doubt believed that Sandy had gotten exactly what she deserved, because, based on the evidence, she apparently *was* a whore just like those sad women that Jack had dispatched in Whitechapel so many years ago.

I never believed that Sandy was a whore, no matter how much evidence to the contrary. I'd *known* her, she'd been my other half. We'd been simpatico. Despite whatever the circumstances seemed to signify, I just knew that Sandy wasn't a whore. I never doubted it for a moment, no matter what everyone else saw, and thought, and knew. This whole thing, this whole situation and its tragic outcome – it was all just the damnedest thing. What it all meant, I couldn't begin to guess, but it didn't mean that Sandy had been a whore, that she'd been deceiving me, doing unspeakable things with low-life men behind my back. Since I knew this in my heart and my mind and my soul to be the truth, the whole thing was all the more baffling to me.

The indelicate and gory details of my wife's murder were blurred in the press. *Blurred* is a nice word – the details were *eliminated* in the press. It turned out that Billy's dad was some sort of big political wheel – I never did find out which car he was on – but he was big enough, and all the rest of them (and those of us left behind) were small enough, that the whole thing never got more than one single article in the paper. Jobs were threatened, unofficial gag orders unofficially ordered – and something that could've – and maybe *should've* – blown up like Wonderland or Cielo Drive just quietly faded into the cold case files.

The one small headline mentioned a drug sale gone awry, with *several shot.*

The consequence of all the details being swept under the bureaucratic rug was that once I transferred to his jurisdiction, I was able to work on the case with Solly. The fact that one of the victims was my wife was ignored, just like all the other gruesome details were ignored. Buried.

It didn't take long to discover that all the girls – Taylor, Pat, Chris, and Cat, just like Sandy – were all from regular, upper-middle-class walks of life. Billy, of course, was from even higher up the social ladder. Grieving families grieved, but they all accepted the explanation that their daughters and sisters had been involved in no wrong doing – they'd simply been in the wrong place at the wrong time.

Apparently, it was not known by, and therefore not mentioned to the grieving families that the ladies had all of a sudden awakened one day and decided to place an ad in the kinky section of the internet. Once it was discovered that the relatives didn't know this unseemly tidbit, it was decided that there was no need to further upset them with the news. Merciful, perhaps, but shoddy police work in my eyes.

I knew. And maybe if someone else had been told, it might've led to some answers.

Even though moms and dads and brothers and sisters had no idea about what had been going on, by tracing back the numbers on Sandy's cell (it'd been her number listed in the ad) we were able to talk to plenty of dudes that'd read the ad and called. But no one still alive had ever made the hook-up, however. Curiously, every single one of the guys we interviewed had an air-tight alibi for the evening in question. So we couldn't suggest that any of them had shown up, didn't want to wait his turn, and had therefore decided to wreak all that havoc.

No one, except for the six unfortunate dudes present, had ever actually met Sandy and her friends. The fatal event seemed to have been a one-time thing. One time, I'd often reflect, apparently had been all that was needed.

The unfortunate young men who'd died, unlike the ladies, hadn't been regular upper-middle-class fellas. I'd guessed as much from one look at Sammy, the lone survivor. Aged nineteen to twenty-four, they were a collection of low-class tough guys. Every single one of them had a record, four for sex-related crimes. All were healthy – *muscular and well-formed,* as the autopsy reports stated – and unexpectedly, I thought, free of hard drugs or disease.

The coroner's report on the crime stated that each of the men had had his *external reproductive organs removed by some unknown means. The removal was accomplished by a method that left behind an almost complete cauterization of the wound.*

Solly and I collared the M.E. and asked him for all this in English. I found him to be a straightforward old guy, once you bought him a drink, and got him away from the morgue and off the record.

"It's like this, Si," he told us, across Presbyterians – the drinks, not the Christians. "And if you say I told you guys any of this, I'll deny it. But here goes: someone cut off these guys' dicks and balls like they were collecting them for further study. All parts of the external organs were gone. The only thing left that made them men was inside: a little piece of vas deferens and a prostate. And then the wound was closed up somehow."

Solly said, "Your report said an almost complete cauterization."

The M.E. waved his hand impatiently. "But it wasn't, boys. Cauterization was more of a description than a procedure here. Nobody cauterizes anything, anymore – there are other methods for closing up wounds, stopping bleeding; antibiotics to prevent infection. Cauterization was medieval stuff – done with a hot piece of metal or something to stop the bleeding. We really still just have the word; the procedure is hardly ever done anymore. We mostly sew stuff up, not burn it.

"That was how this looked, but not how it was done. We should've said *cauterization by unknown chemical means*, but that would've opened a whole 'nother can of worms. It was like something very sharp cut their nuts off, and as it passed through, it left behind something that sealed up the wound. Almost as if it *healed* it. Hardly any blood. Damnedest thing I ever saw."

"But it didn't kill them?" Solly asked.

"No, but they probably would've wished they were dead, eh? These were what we call *bad cuts,* boys. B. A. D. Balls and dick." The M.E. laughed. We did not. "But it wasn't the cause of death. That was from someone jamming an ice pick into the base of their skulls."

I thumbed through the report. "I don't remember any mention of an ice pick."

The M.E. looked at me like I was dumb. "This is all off the record, Si. We didn't actually say that in the report, because the weapon was never recovered. But that's what it probably was. A thin, sharp metal rod jammed into their brains."

The M.E. paused, drained his drink, smiled at us. "Or, if you believe Sammy Mellucci, it was sexy chicks in Darth Vader masks with snakes coming out of them, who burst in and killed all the men with ray guns, after robot chicks with metallic vaginas bit off their dicks." He signaled the waitress for another drink. "I read reports, too, boys."

Sol said, "Sammy said he didn't even realize that his nuts were gone until he looked for them later. He said she only got half of them because he was pulling out when he heard his buddy scream. How could he not feel something like that?"

The M.E. shrugged. "Perhaps she used some kind of anesthetic. Kinda like a mosquito or something."

"Mosquito?" I asked.

Again the M.E. looked at me like I was dumb, and asked, "Didn't you boys ever take biology?"

I said, "Solly majors in biology to this day." Solly didn't even smile. When the M.E. looked confused at my non sequitur, I said, "Never mind, Doc. What about mosquitoes?"

"Female mosquitoes have an anesthetic in their saliva," the M.E. explained. "That's why you don't feel it when they bite you. That's what makes it itch later. Sammy said he didn't feel it when this chick cut off one of his balls and most of his dick. Like you say, how could he not feel that? I'm saying, she had to've had some kind of anesthetic in her mechanical snatch to make it so he didn't feel anything. To make it so he didn't realize what was happening."

Solly said, "Sammy Mellucci is a convicted sex offender, a white supremacist, a suspected rapist, and an all-around asshole."

The M.E. looked at him, smiled again. "What was it that Kevin Costner said in *JFK*? Something about – why does what you are make you a bad witness? Why does it mean that a hooker had to've been mistaken in what she witnessed, just because she's a hooker? Do you see what I'm getting at?"

"Are you saying that you believe that robot hookers chopped off most of Sammy Mellucci's wang?" Solly asked.

"There are more things in heaven and earth . . ." waxed the M.E. philosophically.

"Seriously?" I asked.

The M.E. sighed and leaned forward, lowered his voice. "Look, boys. I've seen a lot of inexplicable deaths in my time. A lot of them. *In-ex-pli-ca-ble*. Beyond explanation. Most times, if there aren't any relatives or media, we just come up

47

with a cause of death that's as close as possible, then tag 'em and bag 'em. We'll just use broad, generalized terms: strangulation, if there are broken blood vessels in the eyes. Blunt force trauma if their skull's bashed in. You know what the caseload is like.

"That's what we did here, what your boss did – just glossed things over a little bit. The men died from puncture wounds to the back of the head. What caused these wounds?" The M.E. shrugged. "The women died from multiple stabs wounds to the abdomen, caused by a thin, serrated blade, or maybe several thin, serrated blades. What was the weapon?" Again he shrugged.

"The details that the men were all castrated and that the women all had giant holes cut right through the abdominal wall into the uterus – none of that got in the paper did it? The paper said they were all shot. What difference does it make how they died? It doesn't make any of them any less dead, does it? Who's gonna talk about it? You? Me?

"And if you notice, they didn't even mention Sammy's name in the paper. The only witness – buried. Where is he, anyway?"

Solly said, "He's up at State. With all the other nuts."

Again the M.E. smiled. "Awaiting trial, perhaps?"

Solly and I exchanged glances. "Something like that."

"Yeah, something like that," the M.E. said. "It's funny how he was never named in the paper in connection with this. No mention of any live ones at all." When we said nothing, he continued. "What I'm saying is this, boys. Something strange happened in that warehouse. Maybe not octopus-faced chicks and robot hookers, but something strange. *In-ex-pli-ca-ble*."

So Sol and I drove up to the State Mental Hospital to talk to once-upon-a-time tough guy, Sammy Mellucci.

Solly drove, and I studied the pictures of Sammy's injury. Whatever the weapon had been that produced it, it hadn't been wielded as efficiently as with the other victims. Sammy had only lost one testicle and about half of his member – a great lengthwise gouge having been smoothly removed from it. I wondered if it still functioned – somehow I doubted it. There was just too much missing. I also wondered if the crazy house doctors had even considered trying to fix him so that he *could* ever use it again as nature intended. Somehow, considering his record for utilizing it in criminal endeavors involving young girls, I doubted that, too.

Sammy was happy to have visitors, and told us his story again. He and his buddy Rusty had talked to some chick online, then on the phone. They'd gone to the warehouse to get laid.

"Rusty hooked up with a little dark-haired chick, and I picked out this redheaded bitch. They had these rooms set up, you guys seen 'em – with beds and stirrups. I thought that was different, so I went in there with Kitty."

Wordlessly, I showed him a picture of Cat and Sandy.

Sammy said, "Yeah, that's her." He tapped Cat's face with his finger. I noticed that his nail was bitten down to the quick. He added, "And the other one was there, too."

"What happened next?" Solly asked.

"I took off my clothes," Sammy replied. "I set my pistol on top of them on some little table or something in there. I don't remember. She put her feet in the stirrups, and I started goin' at her, standing up. And it was good, man, like she was some teenage chick, really tight. I was going to town, when I heard Rusty scream, and I kinda paused on the outstroke, if you dig. I listened for a second, and in that second, I felt something seem to wrap around my balls. I looked down and thought I was hallucinating. Dude, there was this metal thing coming out of her pussy! Some kinda little metal tentacle thing was trying to wrap itself around my balls, and she's moaning, 'Oh, Sammy, come back, I want you inside me!' and reaching up for me with her hand.

"But it was too much for me, man, even if it was just a hallucination, or so I thought at the time. I jumped back and punched her in the jaw."

"And you didn't feel this metal thing cut you?" Solly asked.

Sammy shook his head. "I've been thinking about that all this time. How could I not feel it? But the only thing I can figure is that I must've forgot about my dick when Rusty started screaming, and started concentrating on saving my ass, if you know what I mean. That's the only thing I can think of.

"Haven't you ever been in a fight and not felt the damage 'til it was all over? I got cut up pretty bad one time, and never even felt it until I drove a busted beer bottle into this asshole's cheek, and he finally went down. Fuckin' tweaker.

"Anyway, after he finally went down, I discovered that I was all cut up. But I hadn't felt anything during the fight. I think it must've been something like that."

"Are you trying to convince us, or yourself, Sammy?" Sol asked.

Mellucci looked at him and I noticed a ghost of the fear I'd seen before in his eyes. "A little of both, I guess." He looked over at me, and seemed very young. "I mean, Rusty must've felt it, huh? That's why he started screaming, don't ya think?"

"Maybe he just looked down, like you did," I said. "Maybe he didn't feel it. Maybe he just saw it, like you did."

"So you punch this chick in the mouth," Solly said. "What happened then?"

"I was in the last room, so when I backed out of the curtain, I looked down the row," Sammy said, "But I didn't see Rusty. I saw three other chicks."

"In Darth Vader masks," I said. "According to your statement."

Sammy had a little table in his room, and now he pulled open a drawer in it, and removed a folded piece of notebook paper. He said, "Remember, a few years ago, when that guy kidnapped the ten little girls? Had them all in a room, playing dollies and tea parties? He'd just started tying them up when the Feds busted in on him?"

Sol and I exchanged glances. "Can't say as I remember that one, Sammy," he said.

"Yeah, me either." Mellucci shrugged. "But Styles – that's what he says he's in here for. Maybe he did it. Maybe he made it all up. This *is* a nuthouse, you know." He looked up at us for a second. "On the other hand, there seem to be a lot of us in here for real crimes that no one else seems to've heard about, if you know what I mean. Anyway, he made this sketch for me."

Sammy handed the notebook paper to Solly, who unfolded it and examined it briefly, then handed it to me. I was surprised at the skill wrought by some insane almost child killer – the drawing looked as if it'd been executed by a first-rate anime artist.

"This is what you saw?" I asked.

"Like Styles was there!" Sammy said in satisfaction.

The picture showed a curvy, full-breasted woman in a black leather or latex cat suit, wearing what looked, indeed, like the top part of Darth Vader's helmet. Below where the nose structure would've been were Cthulhu-like tentacles. I handed the drawing back to Sammy.

"Don'tcha wanna make a copy?" Sammy asked. "I know they have a copy machine here somewhere. In the office, maybe?"

"It's okay, Sammy," Solly said and smiled. "I think we'll remember this girl, if we run into her."

"Thanks, Sammy," I said genuinely. "We may be in touch."

"S'okay, dude," Sammy replied. "Stop by any time. I don't get many visitors. Like, none. The docs, they think I cut up all those people. I'm not going anywhere."

Solly cocked his head, intrigued. "You seem okay with that, Sammy."

Sammy shrugged and said, "Three hots and a cot, here, and no Bubba trying to fuck me every time I bend over. But there's still bars on the window here, man. No one's getting out." He flapped the drawing at us. "But then no one like this is getting in, either."

And life went on. The years passed. Solly and I investigated other murders, solved most of them. Others went into oblivion, into the oft-mentioned cold case drawer, right there next to Sandy's case.

My life normalized, as much as it could. Sol was a pillar of friendship, fixing me up with girls, so we could double-date.

Do you think that's wrong, that I dated? Do you think that I should've abstained, and thereby kept the memory of my marriage to Sandy all shining and unsullied? No. Sandy wouldn't've wanted it that way. Sandy saw me as a man, with a man's needs, and she would've seen it as unnatural for a man to forgo a normal life, just because the one true love of his life had been brutally murdered.

But the girls I dated knew. They sensed that something was off about me. They could tell that, even though I was going through all the motions – they knew that the capacity for providing that *real* kind of love (that kind that everyone deserves) – that capacity was already spent in me. I might've seemed like a great guy, and a lot of them told me that I was – sweet, thoughtful, caring, and all that – but after a while, they'd sense that something was missing. They'd realize that no matter how attached I might seem, I wouldn't particularly miss them if they left. So they left.

It never mattered though, because for every one that left, Solomon Nova would scare up two more.

They left him, too, because he had a similar streak. Sol just didn't care, either. Different motivation, same basic how-can-I-miss-you-if-you-won't-go-away attitude. Solly hadn't lost his true love, like I had. Solly had never even *looked* for a true love – he didn't get the concept.

He was like a little kid in the ball pit at *Chuck E. Cheese.* Why hang on to this red ball when there are a million red balls, not to mention blue ones and yellow ones? Besides the difference in color, women were just like balls to Solly – all the same, interchangeable. They were fun to play with, but certainly nothing for him to build his life around, as I'd done with Sandy.

About what happened to Sandy – I think the strangeness of the whole thing had left me perennially wrapped in a kind of numbness. Sure, I missed Sandy, and it was absolutely horrible what had happened to her. And I grieved, and the grief passed, in its season. But I think my loss was always overshadowed by the *why* – the *unknowable, unfathomable why.* The weirdness that had led up to the thing – the sudden lesbianism, then the just as sudden complete reversal into what appeared (to everyone but me) to be some kind of perverse group prostitution – then the horrific, unspeakable slaughter of all of them. The whole situation was so bizarre as to deaden the anger (and even some of the pain) with a kind of hopeless wonder for the longest time.

Not a single lead we received ever panned out. Sometimes, late at night, I'd open the file and look at it. It hadn't stayed long in the cold case cabinet, you see. It was at my place, where I could peruse it at my leisure.

This is what I expect happened to all the missing files belonging to all the other famous unsolved murder cases. They say the Black Dahlia file went missing – and I bet it's still at the back of some long-dead uniform's closet. He just borrowed it to study one day, 'cause he had a hunch. He was gonna crack that case wide open. He grew old, retired, died – and somehow that file never got put back where it belonged, where new eyes might someday look at it.

But no one else would ever be looking for leads in the murder of Sandy and her friends. No James Ellroy would write any novels; no John Gilmore would solve the case through interviews with old nutballs who conveniently confessed and then just as conveniently died. There was no public imagination to be fired by all this horror, because the public had been spared the details from the very beginning.

Some nights, I'd review the file, pore over it, looking for something that I'd previously missed. I knew all the names, all the histories, by heart. There was absolutely nothing to bring all these people together except for a sex ad. None of them seemed good enough or bad enough to prompt someone to massacre them all.

But still I looked at the folder, every now and again. The pictures had ceased to hurt; they'd long ago become only crimes scenes, colors and lights and shadows, elbows and knees and splatters. Like most cops, I believed that all the answers were there in that file – I believed that criminals always leave behind enough evidence to catch them, every time. If only I was clever enough to figure it out.

Solly and I had tried to chase down the three sets of odd shoe prints – two approximately size seven and one size eight – that'd been left in the blood, but they couldn't be matched to any known shoe brand.

I pestered the M.E. to recommend doctors that I could talk to about the strange surgical nature of the castrations, the identical method by which each of the women had been butchered. I exhausted all of them, too, and not a single clue was produced. I learned that *inexplicable* was a medical term.

I experienced a thrilling *ah-ha* moment when I found something new one night in one of the pictures that I'd stared at a million times before. There, under one of the cots, half obscured by a sheet, was Sandy's interstellar egg crate. I even found it in the evidence locker and smuggled it out. I took it around to a bunch of geologists. None of the goop was there anymore – Sandy had washed it out so well, it seemed, that not a molecule of it could be found, not even with a microscope.

And the geologists were not at all surprised when I told them how I'd come by the thing. (I told them that it'd crashed into the road, and didn't elaborate that it had also been a favored keepsake of my murdered wife.) Things fell to Earth all the time, they told me. It was quite large to be such a thing, they said, and it was really a pity that I no longer had the other half – but it really wasn't that unusual.

They flat out didn't believe me when I told them about the eggs that had once been inside. All of those were missing – I even checked with Hansen, Sandy's old boss. He said he'd never received any purple-black ovoids from her. I searched for the eggs in the pictures, but they weren't there.

And so the years passed. The file became yellowed. The haircuts in the dude's mug shots, and the clothing in the pictures of the girls while they were still alive became dated. Solly and I went out with girls, neither of us becoming attached for more than a hot minute here or there. Only our friendship deepened. My dad passed, quickly and mercifully, and Solly only occasionally and derisively mentioned a stereotypical family which he despised, on the East Coast. So after a while, all we had was each other. Brothers didn't have a better relationship.

And then one day, it happened. And as with a lot of life-changing events, there was no fanfare, no warning. If I would've walked out of the office five minutes earlier, I probably would've missed the whole thing, maybe never would've even heard about it.

But as it happened, Solly and I were walking out to the elevators, leaving for lunch. I realized that I'd left my phone on my desk. It wasn't like I was expecting any calls – who was gonna call me? But like a kid, I'd kind of developed a feeling of vulnerability without the thing. So Solly went down to get his car, and I went back to get my phone.

On the way back to my desk, I heard O'Hara say to somebody, "Did you see the pictures? She cut off his dick *and his nuts,* and then just ran off! Took them with her!"

Oh, yeah, something I may not've made clear about Sandy's murder scene. None of the men's missing genitals ever turned up, except for poor Sammy's one testicle and that big chunk that was missing from his dick. They were found squished on the floor under the bed in the bay he'd been in. It was probably one of the crime scene techs that had squished them. My buddy the M.E. told me this in confidence, based on the amount of decay that had set in pre-squishing, or something like that. Still more shoddy police work.

Regardless of how they got squished, the removed parts of Sammy's anatomy were totally unsalvageable, as far as any reattachment may've gone. I don't think that anyone even let Sammy know that they'd been found. The tissue was analyzed for any clues about that pain deadening agent, and the strange means of removal, but all tests proved inconclusive.

But the other five sets of cocks and balls? The Vader-Cthulhu women had apparently taken them all with them.

I walked over to O'Hara's desk, and looked at the file he had open on his computer. He let me page through all the pictures, and sure enough, they showed what was left after some guy had his junk removed, as if by surgery. All that was left was a smooth wound and a couple of little tubes sticking out. The pictures were up close and personal, so I couldn't tell any other details other than that the guy was white.

I told O'Hara that Sol and I'd had an unsolved like this, once – back when he wasn't yet old enough to cross the street by himself. I asked him to email me a copy of the file.

He said, "Sure, Si," and sent the file to me. He said that he doubted there could be any connection, however – this one wasn't going to go unsolved. They knew exactly whodunit; had witnesses and everything.

When I got back to my desk, my forgotten cellphone was ringing, and Solly was asking me where the hell I was. I told him to go pick something up and bring it back – we might have a new lead on an old case.

It took a few favors and promises of favors to get O'Hara to turn the case over to us, but nothing that would make me blush to perform. These kind of investigative personnel switcheroos happen all the time. Specialties are an illusion. All the different division designations are really just administrative window dressing, necessary for payroll and all that. Cops are really just cops, after all.

O'Hara was just a kid, not more than four or five years older than the victim in this case, and I think he was really kind of grateful to get out from under it – the photos and the idea of what'd occurred were playing a little too much on his imagination. And the case had stalled, despite his witnesses and his evidence, and I think he was glad that if it wound up going unsolved after all, it would now be on Solly and me.

I studied the photos. There were differences, sure, but the basic premise of the whole thing was the same. The kid had been castrated, the resulting wound almost identical to the ones sustained by those five dead street toughs (and Sammy Mellucci, too, at least partially) so many years ago.

But Solly took issue with the differences, 'cause Solly was just a contrary kinda guy.

Just like on TV cop shows, his desk was across from mine, and he sat at it in silence, perusing the file on his computer. At last he looked over at me and said, "Okay. Our original women were involved in some sort of group sex thing."

My partner had long ago ceased to worry about any feelings that I might've had about what certainly seemed to be the truth, even if my beloved, at one time seemingly perfect wife was involved. He knew what I believed about the whole situation.

He said, "This was a well-to-do fourteen-year-old girl and another well-to-do eighteen-year-old boy."

I waved my hand in dismissal. "I'm not talking about the players, Sol. Not yet. I'm talking about the wounds, first. Look what I found in the archives."

Sol came around to my desk and was as surprised as I'd been that the old case file had been scanned and was available for viewing. It must've been done sometime before I'd ceased dutifully putting the file back in the cold case cabinet and had just taken it home with me. Some efficient police work, for a change.

I pointed at the screen, where I had a picture of the wound of the new victim side by each with a picture of the wound of one of the old victims.

Solly studied them, and, as I said, he took issue. "Still, they're not exactly the same, my friend." He pointed at the screen. "This new one seems less ragged, healed almost. And those little tubes, there? What is that? They seemed to be better defined here. You can barely make them out in the old picture."

"Those tubes are the kid's vas deferens and his urethra," I informed Solly.

I'd studied the old pictures and the coroner's notes enough that I knew. I'd also looked at diagrams on the internet – I knew as much about the male reproductive system as a urologist or a health-nut homo, at least as far as where the structures were and how they were connected.

I told Solly, "The kid used to pee out of this one and come out of this one, except that they were once connected inside his dick, as one tube. He might still pee out of one of them, someday, I imagine, after a little reconstruction and a little practice. But since he has neither dick nor balls, anymore, I'm not so sure about coming."

Sol feigned amazement. "Is that so? When did you learn so much about anatomy?" But it was a rhetorical question, because Solly was not unaware of my late night studying of old police files, my diagram searches on the internet. "Still," he insisted, "they don't look exactly the same."

I looked at him. "Are you kidding me? They are *exactly* the same. The same kind of cauterization thing, like the doc said, like the wound was being closed at the same time it was being made." I looked at the picture again. "Sure, this one looks a little smoother. Maybe it's just the picture. Maybe it's because the kid isn't dead." I looked at Sol again. "Or, maybe – what's it been, eighteen years? Maybe they've refined their technique."

Solly looked around and lowered his voice for effect. "Now you're talking crazy talk, Si. This girl is only fourteen years old. She wasn't even dreamt of when that other shit went down."

I looked steadily at him. "Maybe ol' Cat taught her."

Sol shook his head. He went back and sat down at his own desk again. "More crazy talk. Cat staggered off somewhere and bled to death. She got stabbed, just like the rest of them."

I said, "We didn't find any evidence of that."

"Yeah, I know. Maybe she held her guts in, and didn't drip. I don't know. But she's dead, man. And if she's not dead, she's somewhere far away from here. She didn't teach anything to a fourteen-year-old rich girl."

I just looked at him across our desks. Sol sighed. He knew that I wasn't going to let this go. Not now, after all these years. It was a break – far-fetched, unlikely, but still a break.

"Who do you want to talk to first?" he asked.

Solly drove to the wealthy side of town, so we could speak to Mr. and Mrs. Dutch, the alleged cutter's parents. And he'd called and made an appointment first. You didn't just show up and knock on the door to these kinds of people's houses. That's how things are different than on TV. They were not accused of any crime. They didn't even have to talk to us. Their underage daughter – she who *was* accused of a crime – was missing, and they were distraught. They had the mayor and the chief on speed dial, and it wouldn't pay to be impolite to them.

While O'Hara and his partner were from Violent Crimes, Solly and I were from Homicide, a fact that he'd failed to mention when he'd made the appointment, because that would've freaked Mom and Dad even more completely out. Like I say, cops are really all just cops, but that word – *homicide* – tends to stick in people's minds. So Solly had just told them that we were fresh eyes on the case and that we wanted to ask a few more questions about some of their daughter's friends and acquaintances. Mrs. Dutch was tired of talking to policemen, but if it might help to find her child, she said she'd be more than happy to speak to us.

On the way over, I read the facts of the case aloud to Solly, in my best Joe Friday voice, just like he liked. "On the evening of May 5th, Officers John Gordon and Phil Spenser respond to an assault call at the home of wealthy businessman Joseph Dutch. They find evidence that a party had been going on at the residence when the crime occurred."

"Party?" Sol grinned at me. "And what kind of party would that be?"

I grinned back at him. "The son was celebrating his eighteenth birthday. Apparently, Mom and Dad were up at the main house, while all the kiddies were carousing down by the pool." I consulted the file. "Assault occurred in a changing room behind the pool. Witness Jonathan Dutch, eighteen – that's her brother, the birthday boy – said he observed his sister, Carly Dutch, fourteen, enter the changing room with the victim, Scott Holland, also eighteen. Witness stated that about ten or fifteen minutes later, he observed his sister flee from the changing room.

"Other witnesses corroborated this description, and added that Carly was visibly upset. Witness Rebecca Cantu, sixteen, stated, 'Carly ran by me. I knew she was crying because her makeup was smeared and running all over her face. Everyone just seemed to freeze for a second when Carly ran by. She was crying and whimpering, staggering up the steps.'

"Assailant ran up the stairs and passed the house, heading for the street. Witness Jonathan Dutch stated that he started to follow her to find out what'd happened when he heard victim screaming.

"Witness Rebecca Cantu stated, 'Everyone seemed frozen when Carly ran by. Then Scotty started screaming, and then everybody was moving, all rushing toward the pool house.' Screaming. Indeed."

Solly asked, "What did the victim say when he stopped screaming?"

I read the file again. "Victim, Scott Holland, eighteen, was incoherent. Medical personnel arrived, sedated him, and transported him. You saw the pictures. What would you say? I'd be incoherent, too." I looked at the file again. "Since admission to the hospital, victim has stated that he remembers nothing about what happened after he entered the changing room with the suspect." I closed the file.

"Seems like a case of young love gone terribly awry to me," Sol said and grinned again. "Where does a fourteen-year-old girl get the skill, not to mention the guts, to cut off some kid's balls?" he asked.

"Like I said," I told him again, "maybe Cat taught her how to do it."

Solly parked the car in front of a ginormous house. "We'll have none of that crazy talk in front of the grieving family." He grinned. "And do me a favor and don't refer to their little girl as *the alleged cutter,* okay?"

"Of course not," I replied, mildly offended. "And that thing about Cat – that's just my pet theory."

"Well, put a leash on it," Sol commanded. "Here we go."

A handsome black woman wearing a maid's uniform ushered us into the den of the Dutch's palatial manse. Mrs. Dutch was still teary, but no longer as hysterical as she'd no doubt been earlier in the investigation. She was obviously medicated. Mr. Dutch just look sad.

Solly introduced us and said, "We'd like to ask you a few more questions about Carly's friends. Anywhere that you can think of that she might've gone, perhaps to hide? Any of her friends that you know of that might try to hide her?"

Mrs. Dutch sighed. "We told all of these things to the other policemen. Carly and all of her friends go to the Zagairre School." Mrs. Dutch caught me consulting the file and explained, "It's an all-girls' prep school. One of the finest in the country."

Sol asked, "Did you know any of Carly's friends from this school, Mrs. Dutch?"

Mrs. Dutch sighed again, failing to disguise her annoyance. "It's a boarding school, Officer –?"

"Nova." Sol smiled at her. "Detective Nova."

Mrs. Dutch smiled faintly back at him. "It's a boarding school, Detective Nova. Carly only comes home on the weekends, and sometimes not even then. Sometimes she stays there right through the weekends. Carly loves Zagairre. But when she does come home, she doesn't bring her friends with her.

"Perhaps Jonathan knows some of her friends. He drives up there to pick her up sometimes." Mrs. Dutch held up one immaculately manicured finger, while dialing her phone with the other hand. "The police would like to talk to you again about your sister's disappearance," she said into the phone, and then hung up. She said to Solly, "My son will be right down."

Jonathan Dutch reminded me of what Solly might've looked like when he was eighteen, if he'd been filthy rich, instead of only good-looking. The kid had the same movie star face, the same effortless confidence. He looked serious – but not *sad,* I noted – and shook our hands as if he was a grown man instead of just an eighteen-year-old kid.

He said, "How can I help you, gentlemen?"

Solly said, "Did you know any of your sister's friends from the Zagairre School, Jonathan?"

Jonathan hesitated for a split second before replying, "Have you visited the scene, yet? Perhaps I can answer your questions on the way down there."

I exchanged glances with Solly. What new development was this? Solly told the kid that that would be a great idea, and Jonathan led us out onto a patio with a stunning, panoramic view of the city, then down flagstone steps to the pool.

The pool house was still draped with crime scene tape, and Jonathan stopped just outside the yellow barrier, as if it was electrified. He asked, "How long do we have to leave this up?"

I looked at the notice attached to the tape. "A few more days," I told him.

Jonathan shrugged and walked a few feet away and perched on top of a stone table, built out of what appeared to be marble. He reached into his pocket, and to my surprise, took out a pack of Kools and lit one. I figured even rich kids had to rebel.

"I know you guys didn't have to come down here with me," he said. "I'm sure you already have pictures of all this." He gestured with the cigarette. "I just didn't want to talk about it in front of Mom."

Now that he was sure he had our attention, Jonathan leaned forward and lowered his voice. "Some of those girls at the school where my sister goes are really slutty. I've talked a couple of them into blowing me in the car while I was waiting for Carly to get out of class. I don't even remember their names."

Jonathan grinned, displaying perfect teeth. Crazily, I heard Sandy's voice in my head – *His dentist must be so proud!* – something she said whenever she saw someone with great teeth.

Solly and I didn't exchange glances after Jonathan's last remark, because that was exactly what the kid wanted – he wanted us to look at each other as if we might disapprove, or as if we might be shocked, or even as if we might be impressed. Any reaction would do – so we made sure not to give him one. Not yet.

Solly just smiled blandly at the kid. "What exactly are you trying to tell us, Jonny?"

Jonathan leaned forward a little further. "What I'm trying to tell you is that, when they do find Carly, and she tries to say that she was raped, or that she was acting in self-defense, or something like that – what I'm trying to tell you, is maybe they're teaching them a little *How to Be a Slut 101* up there at Zagairre, and maybe any rape claims would be ridiculous."

Solly affected his best confused Columbo look and said, "Could you run that by me again?"

Jonathan thought he was smarter than us, so he was eager to cooperate. There was no way we were going to fool *him*. So why not tell us what he thought we needed to hear? But I knew he was no match for Solly, no matter how much rich-boy confidence he had. Solly would get him to cough up everything he knew, whether it would be in his best interest to tell us or not.

Jonathan said, "Look, gentlemen. I was standing right here. I saw her go in there with Scotty. There was no coercion. There were no threats. In fact, I'd testify that Carly *led* him in there." He sucked on his Kool, then added, "*By the hand.*"

"That doesn't mean he didn't try to rape her," Sol said. "After they got inside, maybe she changed her mind. *No means no,* and all that."

Jonathan stared at the water in the pool. It was absolutely still. He was quietly adamant when he said, "Scotty is no rapist. He's my best friend, and I'm telling you, *he's no rapist.*" He took another long drag on his Kool. "Besides, Carly loves him. She's loved him for years. Since we were kids."

"Still," I said, "she could've changed her mind once she got in there with him. *A woman's prerogative . . .*"

63

Jonathan looked at me and rolled his eyes at that worn-out chestnut. "She wouldn't've said no," he said, swinging his legs and kicking absently at the bench to the marble table. "She must've cut him 'cause she's just a crazy bitch. I told my mother, that's what she gets for –"

Solly interrupted the kid, chiding, "That's not a very nice thing to say about your sister."

Now Jonathan looked at Sol like *he* was stupid and said slowly, "I told my mother, that's what she gets when she adopts some stranger. Who knows what kind of crazy genes Carly has?"

I consulted the file again. There was no mention that Carly was adopted.

"So, you don't think of Carly as your sister?" I asked, stating the obvious.

"No, man. I never have." Jonathan snuffed out his cigarette on the underside of the marble table, then carefully discarded the butt in a nearby shrub, taking pains to hide it.

Solly asked, "When did your parents adopt Carly?"

Again Jonathan looked at my partner like he was stupid. "When she was a baby." He put his fingers up like quotation marks. "*Just a few hours old*, as the heartwarming tale goes."

Since Jonathan kept looking at him like he was stupid, Sol acted stupid. "So, you're what – three years older than Carly?"

Jonathan lit another cigarette and stared at the pool. "Four," he said.

Sol said, "So, your parents adopted Carly when she was a newborn, and you were four. But you don't look at her as your sister?"

Jonathan snapped his gaze back to Sol. "Don't you think I don't love her, or that I'm jealous of her or anything like that. I do love her. It's just that I've never felt very . . . *brotherly* toward her. We've always been more like . . . like *friends,* I guess." His eyes drifted back to the pool again. "I've always tried to tell her, 'We're not really related, not like blood, like real brothers and sisters or anything, so there's no reason why we can't . . .'" Jonathan's attention suddenly returned to Sol, who waited patiently, curiously, for him to complete his unguarded, stream-of-consciousness sentence. No, Jonathan wasn't nearly as smart as he thought he was. "There's no reason we can't be friends," he concluded quickly.

Solly let all this potential weirdness slide and asked, "Tell us about Scott Holland. You say he's your best friend?"

Jonathan once again surveyed the motionless water, not looking at us. "I've known Scotty since the 5th grade. I'm sure you've already seen pictures of him. We're about the same size, but he's blonde, while I have dark hair. He always looked like he could be Carly's brother more than me."

Jonathan took another drag on his Kool. "Carly decided that she was in love with him when she was twelve. Scott was never interested – hell, we were sixteen when she was twelve. I'd give him a hard time about it, tell him she sure didn't look twelve, now did she? She looked sixteen – hell, she could pass for eighteen now.

"But Scotty was an oak. He wasn't having any. *'She's twel-lov-a!'* he would say, making a three syllable word out of it. If I was him, it wouldn't've mattered that she was twelve, 'cause she surely didn't look it. But back then, he was just not interested."

"But what about now?" I asked. "She's not twelve anymore – you say she could pass for eighteen."

Again, Jonathan's gaze snapped back from his contemplation of the still waters of the pool. "Yeah, now," he said and shook his head. "She most certainly is not twelve anymore. It's been awhile since I've seen hear – since Christmas. My mother sends us to these boarding schools – I'm graduating next month from Simmerton."

Jonathan waited for a reaction after dropping the name of the exclusive school. When he received none, he shrugged and continued. "Anyway, this past week – it was the first time in a while that we were all home together. Me and Scotty. And Carly."

Again his gaze softened and drifted away. "I couldn't believe how different she looked since Christmas – how . . .

grown up she is now. And right away, as soon as I walk in the door, she starts asking me about Scott, when is he coming over, does he have a girlfriend, and all that. It was obvious that she still had a crush on him."

Jonathan took a quick puff on his Kool. "I told Scotty how much she was asking about him, and he said. 'No way, she's only fourteen!' But then he saw how beautiful she is, how grown up she is. The three of us hung out together that first afternoon, watched movies.

"As soon as she left the room, he asked me if I thought she'd *go out with him.*" Sarcastic emphasis on the last four words. "So much for her being only fourteen."

"So, you arranged this." Solly gestured at the crime scene tape. "This little rendezvous."

Again, Jonathan looked sharply at him. "Who told you that? You can't prove that. I know that you haven't talked to either of them – Carly's gone, and Scotty is . . . Scotty is . . . Scotty's still in the hospital."

Jonathan took a deep breath and looked from Sol to me and then back to Sol again. He realized that he'd made an error, that he'd overreacted to an innocent question. He let the breath out. "Yeah, I arranged it. She kept bugging me about him. 'Oh, he's so cute!' and all that shit."

Jonathan flicked his cigarette into the pool, just to hear it sizzle, I think, just to make the water move, even if it was just a tiny bit. Then he thought better of it and fetched a skimmer and plucked it out.

"What about Scotty?" I asked. "Did he bug you about it, too?"

Jonathan dropped the butt in the same hiding bush as the first one and put the skimmer back. He sat on the table again and rolled his eyes. "Oh, yeah. After he saw her again, he wanted me to fix them up right away. I mean, what guy wouldn't want to get at her if he could? Especially since he knew how Zagairre girls are . . ."

"You told him how they are?" Solly asked. "You told him about those two that blew you in the parking lot? Did you tell him that maybe your little sister had gotten to be that way, too?"

Helplessness, pain and remorse flashed in Jonathan's eyes. But they were immediately replaced by a cold defiance. "I might have. What of it?"

Solly shrugged. "Nothing. I'm just trying to gauge what Scott's expectations might've been when he went into that changing room with your fourteen-year-old sister. Can you shed any light on that, Jonny?"

Jonathan's expression remained defiant. "I don't know what he expected. To get some, I imagine. I imagine that's what she expected, too. How was I to know that she was going to go all crazy on him and cut his nuts off?"

"And his dick," I calmly reminded Jonathan. "She cut off his nuts *and* his dick, and apparently took them with her to wherever she's gone."

Jonathan swallowed hard at my cold recitation of the awful facts, and now he looked like a kid to me, just a scared kid, despite his good looks and his perfect teeth and his money and his manners. All the confidence that'd made him seem older had fled.

"Where did she even get a knife?" he asked us in astonishment.

Still calmly, I said, "Wherever she got it, she took that with her, too."

Abruptly, Solly said, "You think you could show us Carly's room, Jonny?"

The kid nodded, swallowed again. He seemed to get a hold of himself. We silently followed him up the flagstone steps and back into the immense house. Mom and Dad were still where they had been, and Jonathan mumbled something about taking us up to see Carly's room. We paused for their permission, and when they nodded, we followed him up a back staircase to the second floor.

Carly's room looked as you might expect a wealthy, pampered fourteen-year-old girl's room to look: it was pink and pinker; there was a painting of a unicorn on one wall.

Curtains surrounding a white four-poster made it appear to be draped in cotton candy. There was still a toy box in the closet.

Sol pushed the eject button on the Blu-ray player – *The Little Mermaid* slid out. He looked at me, then turned and said to Jonathan, "Do you think she hides her sex toys under the bed?"

Jonathan started as if slapped, but immediately regained his smarts. He shrugged. "They're probably at school. With the other girls'."

Now Solly looked at me and squinted a little bit, making sure that Jonathan could read his reaction this time: *I'm not buying it.* I nodded – this was obviously a little girl's room, not the lair of some teenaged man-eater.

Then I remembered that she'd turned Scott Holland into a eunuch with one stroke, and maybe I wasn't so sure, after all.

Just like on TV, Sol produced a card and handed it to Jonathan. He said, "If you think of anything else that might be useful, give us a call."

Jonathan peered at the card, as if it was written in Sanskrit. Still reading the small print, he offered me his hand. I shook it. He put the card in his pocket and shook Sol's hand, then he led us down the sweeping front staircase and out the huge front door.

Pausing on the stones steps, I asked him. "Where do you think she is, Jonathan?"

Genuine puzzlement crossed his striking features. "I have no idea. The police, you guys, already checked with the school, all her friends. She can't even drive! She just ran out into the night, barefoot, and disappeared."

"Call me if you think of anything," Solly said again, and we left.

As we headed back to the office, I said to Solly, "You go first."

Solly grinned that woman-killing smile, so similar to the one possessed by young Jonathan Dutch. "I've got a question for you, Si. What's the difference between a bitch and a whore?"

I shrugged, shook my head.

Sol's grin widened. "A whore gives it to everybody. A bitch gives it to everybody but you."

Unaccustomed to this level of vulgarity from him, I frowned. "You're not saying that you think Carly is a . . ."

"No," he said, his grin fading. "Little Carly is neither a bitch nor a whore. But that's not how my close personal friend Jonny sees it."

I wondered what the hell he was getting at now. "Do tell," I said.

Sol looked at me like Jonathan had looked at him – like I was dumb. "Jonny's obviously got more than a little yen for his sister, Si, my friend. You didn't get that? What did he say? *'I've always tried to tell her, "We're not really related, so there's no reason why we can't . . .?"'*

Sol paused to let that sink in for a minute. "I think brother Jonny might've even put the moves on her last week when she got back from school. Or maybe even earlier. I don't think he'd force her, so I don't think it got to anything physical. You saw that room – she might not've even known what something physical was, yet.

"I'm sure of it, Si – brother Jon made some kind of pass at Carly, some kind of suggestion of an incestuous nature, if you get my drift – and even though they're not really brother and sister, Carly demurred, because she's just not interested in him. She's interested in his blonde friend.

"So Carly turns him down, and Jonny's pissed now. He's jealous. It's not that she's pure and virginal, in his eyes – he might've thought that before, if she'd only just turned *him* down. But, no – she turns him down, but still asks about his friend.

"And Jon, he thinks, why not me, what's wrong with *me* – why would she want his buddy, someone that looks just like her? Why not him? It's obvious from listening to him talk that he's wanted her for a minute – maybe he's wanted her all his life. After all, they're not really related, right?

"So brother Jon, maybe he thinks he'll get even with her for rejecting him. He sets up this little grope session in the pool house, telling his pal how hot to trot she is. Maybe Jonny figures Carly might slap Scott and not like him anymore if he gets too handsy. Or even better, if she goes through with it, Jonny'll narc her off to Mom and Dad. They'll be ashamed of her, and she'll have to turn to him for comfort. Maybe she'll get pregnant and be further disgraced. That would show her, wouldn't it?"

I was skeptical. I said, "And so?"

Sol was a little miffed that I wasn't enthusiastically embracing his scenario. He said, "I'm telling you, Si. There's something twisted about that little bastard Jonathan."

I shrugged. "Maybe. But neither he nor lover-boy Scotty figured that little Carly would defend herself the way she did. I think we need to go to the hospital."

Solly agreed, and we drove to the upscale private hospital where Scott Holland was convalescing, because, of course, his parents were wealthy, also. Birds of a feather and all that. Since he was eighteen, we didn't need his parents to be present when we interviewed him. Which was good, because they weren't there anyway. A nurse discreetly told Solly that they were hurrying back from Rome at that very moment, so that they could offer comfort to their mutilated boy.

We knocked on the door, and Scott Holland told us to come in. We introduced ourselves.

He was like a photonegative of Jonathan; the same All-American beauty, only reversed. Same perfect teeth, same healthy build. Only Scott was fair, where Jon was dark. I imagined that Scott had possessed the same entitled confidence as his friend – at least until recently, that is. He sat with his hospital bed in the upright position, the blankets pulled up to his chest.

Gently, I asked, "Can you tell us what happened, Scott?"

He looked straight ahead and shook his head. "I don't remember anything."

More to the point, Solly asked, "Why were you in the changing room with Carly?"

Scott said, "She lost her towel. I was trying to help her find her towel." He wouldn't look at either of us.

Now Solly smiled at me. This one was going to be even easier to crack than Jonny – this one *started off* lying.

Sol said, "Oh, I get it, Scott, my friend. You're worried about how all this looks – an eighteen-year-old *man* and a fourteen-year-old *child* enter a dark room together. The eighteen-year-old man comes out sans dick, while the fourteen-year-old child runs off screaming into the night, not to be found. You're worried about how all that reflects on *you*."

Scott Holland just looked straight ahead.

I said, "Look, Scott, we're from Homicide." Now he glanced up at me and blanched white as his sheet. "We're not here to try to bust you on some statutory rape beef. There were some murders, and the men . . . The men wound up just like you, except that they also go an ice pick to the back of the skull.

"So, I don't care about the fact that you're eighteen and she's fourteen. I couldn't possibly care less about that. I want to hear about what happened, so I can see if there's any connection between these incidents."

Scott blinked rapidly at me and said, "You think Carly k-k-killed somebody?"

Solly looked at me, but said to Scott, "It's doubtful, but the method is . . . similar."

"We're trying to see if there could be any connection," I told the kid. "It's very important to us to solve these murders." *Way more important than you could ever know*, I thought. "So my partner and I aren't concerned that the alleged cutter was underage. So you have my word – everything you tell us about anything you did of a sexual nature – it's all off the record. When the boss asks what you said, we'll just tell him, 'He doesn't remember anything.'

"But I need you to tell us, Scott, so that this never happens to anybody else."

Scott swallowed. "I can trust you guys?" he asked.

Sol and I nodded.

"Good," Scott said, "'cause I gotta tell someone. Fucking Jon, he doesn't even want to know what happened. He said he was sorry that his sister did this to me, but all of a sudden he doesn't want to hear anything about it. He's only been in here to see me once, and he couldn't even look me in the eye while he was here."

"That's all guilt, Scott," Solly told him.

Scott smiled tightly, and swallowed again. "Guilt? You bet your sweet ass, it's guilt. This is all his fault. He talked me into it. He said that all Carly ever talked about was how much she loved me and how much she wanted to fuck me. Jon said that it was driving him crazy listening to her talk about me, so would I just do her and get it over with, so she'd shut up.

"She seemed so sweet. I couldn't believe that she talked like that to Jon, but he said that she did, and I don't have any sisters, so what do I know? And Jon was always telling me that all the girls that went to Zagairre were slutty, from the younger ones like Carly, right up through the seniors.

"So he's telling me all this, and I had a few beers, and he keeps talking about it, and talking about it. And then, he brings her down the steps, and she is so hot . . ."

"She doesn't look fourteen at all," Solly said.

Scott looked at him, then back at me, then straight ahead again. "No, she didn't look fourteen, not at all," he said. "She was so beautiful . . . so *sexy*. And then she was talking to me, and Jon nodded at the pool house, and then disappeared back up the steps.

"We were alone, and then we were holding hands, and then we went in there. It was dark, but there was still some light coming in through the windows. There was a table – like you use when you get a massage? First she sat on the end of it. I was standing up in front of her, and we started making out. She wasn't saying no, then.

"I reached under her dress and pulled down her panties. She straightened her legs out to make it easier for me to get

72

them off. She wasn't saying no, then. They caught on her foot and ricocheted up into the rafters somewhere. We laughed about that."

That's why they weren't on the evidence list, I thought. They were still there. No one thought to look up. More shoddy police work.

Scott was saying, "So after a while, I hiked up her dress and squatted down in front of the table and went down on her." He glanced at Solly, who smiled mildly at him. "She was digging that, too, not saying no, then, no sirree, wrapping her legs around my shoulders. Then she laid back and gripped the edge of the table with her toes, her ass and everything else right there by the end. After a few minutes of her squirming around and pulling my hair, I stood up and took off my shorts. I just laid my dick on her, right there where her thigh joins. She got scared, tried to sit up, but I calmed her down. I said I'd just . . ."

"Just put the tip in?" Solly suggested.

Again Scott looked at him and then back at me.

"Who's telling this story?" I said sharply to Sol, then nodded at Scott to continue.

Scott said, "Well, he's right. That's what I said. I told her that I'd just put the tip in, just for a second."

Solomon Nova winked at me.

Scott continued. "She seemed okay with that. She didn't say no or anything. So I eased into her. About halfway, she starts to say, 'No, no, I don't want to! Take it out!' And . . ." Scott looked at me again. "And I swear to God, Mister, I was doing what she asked, I was backing out, when all of a sudden, I felt a little tug, and then it felt like I just *fell out.* It was an odd feeling, so I looked down and there was . . . There was . . . *nothing there!*

"I jumped back and switched the light on – that's how freaked out I was – I didn't care if someone saw us. I looked down again, and there was nothing there! There was a little bit of blood sprayed across my thigh, not much. I looked at Carly – she was sitting up and looking at me now – and there was a little blood on the hem of her dress. I said, 'What did you do to me?'

"I guess I sorta lunged back toward the table and she screamed and jumped up. She ran by me, and was gone."

"Did you see the weapon?" Solly asked.

"See it? I didn't even feel it!" Scott looked at me in agony. "Why did she do this to me? I stopped! I stopped as soon as she asked me to!"

"I don't know why she did it, Scott," I said lamely. How does one comfort a young man with such a grievous injury?

Solly shrugged, and said philosophically, "Why do they do anything they do?"

I glared at him, feeling that this was a spectacularly unfeeling thing to say to a maimed eighteen-year-old boy, one who might never get to find out why women do what they do ever again. Solly just shrugged in answer to my glare.

Scott took a few deep breaths and got a hold of himself again. I thought that he was amazingly calm and in control for a young man with such an injury. *He's probably sedated,* I thought.

At last, he asked, "You said that she might've done this to someone else?"

"No, not her," Solly replied. "The other incident – it was a long time ago. But it was the same way."

Scott looked at him and said, "You mean, like, you think someone taught her how to do this?"

"Something like that," I said, feeling vindicated that someone else could follow my train of thought. I patted him on the shoulder. "What did the doctor say?"

He shrugged and said, "Something about reconstruction. He was really trying to be upbeat, Mister, but I got the impression that he was lying to me."

Before I could respond, Solly slapped the invalid none too gently on the shoulder and said, "Well, hell, kid! Maybe they'll make it twice as big!"

Both of us looked at him incredulously, and the awkward silence lengthened. At last I handed Scott my card, and mouthed the stock line. "If you think of anything else, give me a call."

Solly nodded at that and slid out the door without opening his big mouth again. I patted Scott on the shoulder again, wished him good luck, and also left.

Solly was already waiting for me in the car. When I got in, he said with his usual directness, "If you ask me, it kinda looks like the kid got exactly what he deserved. What do you think?"

I looked back at the hospital as we pulled away, and did not reply.

When I didn't speak immediately, didn't agree with him immediately, as was usually the case, Sol continued. "I think shit like this happens every day, Si. Little girls – they see so much big girl stuff on TV, in the movies. They think they might want to give it a try. Then, being little girls after all, they get scared. Change their minds in the middle.

"But kids like ol' Scott, there – he's not the type to allow little girls like Carly to change their minds. *You've come this far, honey, now you're gonna go at least another six or seven inches farther.* That's his philosophy."

Sol looked over at me. "I think ol' Scott probably just went ahead and slammed it on home, regardless of what she said, regardless of what she wanted, and she cut him prior to the backstroke."

I continued to look silently out the window. At last I said, "I don't think you have the slightest idea what you're talking about, Sol. When has any woman ever told you no? When have any of them ever even told you just maybe?"

Sol shrugged, didn't even smile. "Come to think of it, it is kind of just a concept to me." Then he grinned faintly. "I've had a few pretend to say no, but then when I said, 'Okay, no is fine, too,' then the no turned into a yes."

I told him, "Yeah, and not every eighteen-year-old kid has that kind of depthless self-control, Sol. To wait for a *no* to turn into a *yes*. I know I didn't at that age." I was still not amused. "Maybe Carly did go along for a while, then maybe she did change her mind. But how far is too far, Sol? How far is too late to change your mind?"

Solomon Nova, my partner of some eighteen years, was shocked into seriousness by this statement on my part. He said softly, amazed at my callousness, "No always means no, Si."

"Right," I said a little too loudly, irritated. "But maybe she shouldn't've gone in there with him if she was gonna change her mind."

Sol looked over at me in further surprise. "Are we blaming the fourteen-year-old victim, now?"

I frowned in annoyance. "No. But this kind of shit is never as black and white as it seems. And in this particular case, it seems that the fourteen-year-old might not be the only victim, huh? Scott and his lack of a dick looked a little victimized to me, too."

Solly seemed to consider all this for a minute. "Yeah, maybe Carly shouldn't've gone in there with him. What did she think he wanted to do in there, play checkers? But stupidity isn't a crime, especially not in young girls."

Still, I didn't look at him. "Maybe it should be."

"Jesus Christ, Si, you're a throwback!" Sol said in amazement. "You're a fucking Neanderthal! Women have all the power nowadays, my friend, and absolutely none of the responsibility. They can walk around naked, and if you look at them for too long, then you're sexually harassing them."

I continued to look out the window. "They've always had all the power, Sol. At least with everyone but you."

He let that remark slide by. "We're not talking about some brittle businesswoman, here, Si. This was a little girl, *a fourteen-year-old girl,* and maybe you should cut her a little slack for changing her mind. Maybe she decided in the middle of it that all the fantasies of happily-ever-after that she'd been dreaming of in that pink bedroom didn't equate with a rough standing-up fuck in a hot changing room."

Sol glanced over to see how his further vulgarity was sitting with me. I looked mildly at him and shrugged. He continued. "Maybe Big Man on Campus back there should've gone with his original instinct and let it alone. Sure, nothing is ever black and white. She's exceptionally pretty, she looks a lot older than fourteen. Her twisted brother was there, egging ol' Scotty on, telling tales about the slutty Zagairre Schoolgirls, and all that shit. But still, I say that he shoulda thought. He shoulda took a deep breath, stepped back, remembered that no matter how she looks, she's only fourteen, for Christ's sake, and kept it in his pants."

I sighed and said, "I'm sure that he'll come to that very conclusion every day for the rest of his life, Sol, reconstruction or no. It's just so fucked up – I don't see this kid as some kind of frothing at the mouth rapist. I believe that he didn't force Carly, even if you don't." I paused, then said, "I've seen some that deserve to be castrated like that, sure."

"Like maybe Sammy Mellucci?" Sol said.

"Yeah," I agreed. "Sammy probably deserved it. If not for what he got it for, he probably deserved it for something he'd done in the past. But not this kid. He didn't deserve it, no matter what you say."

We drove in silence for a while, then I remembered Sol saying that maybe Carly hadn't been down for a *standing-up fuck in a hot changing room*. I snapped my fingers. "I just noticed something, Sol. They were all in the same position – Scott, Sammy, probably all those dead dudes. They were all standing up when the axe fell, if you will. Did you notice that?"

Sol shrugged, noncommittal. "I didn't notice."

Then a new idea struck him. "Maybe this is some new wave of feminism. Some new empowerment of women. Empowerment through castration." He looked over at me. "Hell, you could even say the first ones were empowered, right? They set the whole thing up for themselves, for whatever reason."

Sol and I had long ago discovered that the whole warehouse sex scene had been masterminded by Sandy – her name was on the receipts for the ads, the furniture rentals, and the lease (for only one month) of the warehouse. There'd been no shadowy pimp, *no man,* calling the shots.

I looked back at Sol doubtfully, and said, "Yeah, they were all empowered, all right. Right up until the moment someone butchered them. Yeah. Empowered. *You've come a long way, baby.*" I went back to looking out the window again.

We drove in silence for several minutes this time, before Sol said, "What was it you said about this little girl, Si? That maybe someone taught her?"

I looked over at him in mild surprise – he'd called that idea crazy talk, earlier. "Yeah, I said that."

"Perhaps we should pay a visit to Slut School and find out just exactly what they *are* teaching up there. What d'ya say?" Sol asked and grinned at me. "I doubt that it's *How to Be a Slut 101,* but it is a boarding school, right? Plenty of places to hide a little girl in a boarding school, right? Her own boarding school?"

I nodded and Sol made a completely illegal U-turn, ignored the angry honks, and headed for the freeway.

"Do you know how to get there?" I asked in surprise.

"Of course, Simon," he replied. "I pass by there every Thursday on my way to polo practice. Get me some directions, will ya?"

I complied, and he pointed our dusty, government-issue Ford toward the prestigious Zagairre School.

If you Googled high-end private schools for serious-minded young women, you got Zagairre at the top of the list. After I gave Solly the directions to the place, for the forty-five minute ride up there, I learned about the place.

Their meticulously professional website showed an imposing, ivy-covered mansion, and informed me that the School (always capitalized) had once been the pre-income-tax estate of some turn-of-the-century robber baron. The main house had been converted into classrooms and dormitories. The acres of grounds also boasted tennis courts, an Olympic-sized swimming pool, polo field and stables, and a state-of-the-art computer and multimedia center.

I read aloud to Sol, "Any young woman who feels that she meets our exceptional standards is welcome to apply for acceptance. Grades 7 through12."

I clicked through the site as if I was a prospect, or the parents of a prospect. I noted that the tuition encompassed many zeros, and there was no mention anywhere of financial aid. Apparently, each young woman was evaluated and either accepted or dismissed by a three member panel consisting of Zagairre staff.

When we rolled up the lane to the Zagairre School, the first thing that struck me was how the place embodied every single private girls' school cliché imaginable. Behind massive, guard-controlled, wrought iron gates, the campus was a tree-lined study in opulent, almost old-world academe. Members of the student body, all conservatively dressed in uniforms color-coded to their grade-level, strolled the shaded lanes. The occasional faculty member sauntered by, her pace a bit quicker than the students, but not wanting in grace and equally conservative dress.

In other words, there was not a slut to be seen.

We parked and walked up the imposing stone steps of the administrative wing. In the foyer, the gleam from a colossal chandelier was reflected as a warm glow by the immaculate parquet floor. When we approached her desk, a strikingly beautiful young woman, her uniform indicating that she was a senior, rose and asked how she could help us.

We were in Womanland, and even if it was a far more upscale neighborhood of Womanland than the bars and clubs he was used to, it was still time for Solomon Nova to do all the talking. He smiled at the lovely teenager and discretely showed his badge, asking if it might be possible for us to speak to the dean. She smiled back at him and indicated that the dean's office could be found at the top of the stairs.

I immediately noticed that something was wrong. For the first time in our entire acquaintance, here was a woman that seemed to be immune to Solly's inestimable charm. She smiled back, true, and was polite, but that tiny something extra that I never failed to notice in women, young and old alike, when he was talking to them, that little gleam that always indicated a further interest? That was absent this time. When we got to the top of the marble staircase, I looked down at the young woman. She'd resumed her tasks, was not watching Sol as they always did. Strange.

"Did you notice anything odd about that girl?" I asked him.

"You mean the gay one?" he said, and didn't even smile.

"How do you know she's gay?" I asked suspiciously.

Now Solly smiled, just a little. "Trust me. I can just tell these things."

Coming from anyone else but him, it would've just been a cop-out – sure, any woman that doesn't notice you has got to be gay. But he was probably right, probably knew what he was talking about, as I'd never seen such a thing happen before.

The anteroom to the dean's office overlooked the great circular driveway in front of the school. I gazed out the windows at the expensive cars ranged around it, while again Solly spoke. He asked if we might speak to the dean, and the dean's secretary, another lovely senior, said she was sorry to inform us that we'd just missed Miss Catarina, the Director.

What a shame, I thought absently, and continued to look out the window, while the young woman told Sol that Miss Catarina wasn't the dean, but the Director, that they didn't use the term *dean* here at the Zagairre School. She went on to say that while Miss Catarina's schedule was quite full for the afternoon, she'd be more than happy to make us the first ones on Miss Catarina's to-do list for the following day.

When the young woman said *Miss Catarina* for the fourth time, I watched, dumbfounded, as Cat Miner walked down the front steps and stepped into a limousine waiting at the head of the drive.

I blinked, convinced that it had to be some kind of hallucination induced by the incantation of that name, repeated four times. But no, it was definitely her. There could be no mistaking it – the same flaming red hair (*she must be dyeing it these days,* I thought, as I'd seen more than a few grays in the mirror myself). But even after eighteen years, I couldn't mistake that kicking body, even draped in a conservative business suit.

"Yes," I said to the secretary, interrupting Sol mid-word. "We'll take Miss Catarina's first available appointment tomorrow. Please put down that Detective Solomon Nova would like to see her regarding a student, Miss Carly Dutch." I looked at Solly, who was nonplussed at my uncharacteristic interference. "Show the young lady your ID, Detective."

He did so, still looking incredulously at me. The secretary made Solly an appointment for ten o'clock the next morning. As we turned to go, I asked her, "Do you have any kind of bios on the staff that we could look at? Perhaps something you hand out to parents of perspective students?"

The lovely young woman opened a desk drawer and handed me a brochure. I told her thanks and goodbye and led a still speechless Solly out of the room by his elbow.

As we started down the grand staircase, Sol said, "You know what, Si? I think that one's gay too."

I was not concerned with his perceptions of sexual orientations at the moment. I handed him the brochure and said, "You said I was talking crazy talk. I've got some crazy talk for ya. Look in there. Look at the picture of Miss Catarina, the Director."

Sol opened the brochure and then stopped in the middle of the staircase, so abruptly that young women going up and down had to step aside to avoid running into him. He looked up at me and after a few seconds started moving again.

"How did you know it was her?" he asked in astonishment.

"I didn't know it was her," I replied. "I had no clue it was her, even when her secretary kept saying her name over and over, like a curse. I made no connection at all, until I just happened to look out the window and saw her getting into a limo in the driveway at that exact moment."

Solly shook his head and said, "It's a small world after all."

It's a small world after all, indeed, and here I must quote Kipling: "Pause you who read this, and think for a moment of the long chain of iron or gold, of thorns or flowers, that would never have bound you, but for the formation of the first link on one memorable day."

The first link, I guess, that led me to all the bombs here placed was forged the next day when I kept the appointment that Sol and I had with Miss Catarina. By myself. Sol had called me on his way in and told me that he'd been involved in a minor fender bender, and there was no way he was going to be able to make it up to Zagairre by ten o'clock.

I asked him what the hold-up was – he was a cop for Christ's sake, couldn't he get himself out of a simple accident? He said, "It's complicated, my friend. Can you call over to Zagairre and reschedule our appointment?"

I told him that I would, and that I'd call him back with the rescheduled time. I pushed the button on my phone to call, then just as quickly changed my mind, put my phone back in my pocket. Out of nowhere, on the spur of the moment, any expression you choose, I'd decided to just go ahead and keep our appointment with Cat. All by myself.

The secretary, a different girl from the day before, announced me as Detective Nova because that's what it said on her calendar, and that's who I told her I was. I heard Cat's familiar voice over the intercom (*We've scheduled quite the little party, you see, me and the girls*) tell her to show me in.

She was seated at her computer, and before her eye left the screen, she pasted a smile on her face and started to say, "What can I do for you, Detective?" But when she saw it was me, the smile fell away and she sobbed.

"Oh, my God, Si!" she croaked, and the fat tears instantly rolled down her cheeks. She arose from the desk, came around and hugged me, repeating, "Oh, my God, Si!" over and over again.

I've described Cat's reaction to seeing me. Now allow me to describe my reaction to seeing her, hugging her – and may God have mercy on my soul. When she looked up from her computer and met my eyes, I felt an electricity skewer me right through the balls. She didn't look a day older than the last time I'd seen her. If anything, she looked better – slimmer, smoother, more sophisticated. I stood transfixed, paralyzed, unable to move. When she stood up, I saw some pornographic vision, a clip from one of those movies where the remarkably sexy lady executive in the business suit soon takes off her expensive, well-cut clothes and starts doing the most unbelievable things. I blinked. Of course, Cat didn't look like that – she was wearing a very unadventurous, high-collared white blouse, neither shimmery nor see-through, and a Navy blue, A-line shirt that dove several inches below the knee, and not even high heels.

Yet somehow, even the sob, the tears – stroked me. When she came around the desk and embraced me, I was plunged into the miasma of her. Her scent, just enough soap and perfume and women smell, was blended perfection. Her body, soft and hard in all the right places, wracked against me as she sobbed. I hugged her back, and uncontrollably, like a schoolboy, I felt the erection begin. She was molded to me – such a flawless fit – I had to grab her by the upper arms and move her away from me before she could feel it, too. Every animal, monkey part of me screamed in protest – this was what I wanted, *needed*, had to have, pliant quintessential femaleness, all concavities and convexities opposite to my own, all yin to my yang, the pluperfect *other*.

Where in the hell was this coming from? This was the enemy, the only one to escape that bloodbath, the one that had called me and told me it was going to happen, the one I'd been searching for, for eighteen years.

I looked into the huge, depthless brown eyes, and gave her a little shake. "What happened that night, Cat?"

Then somehow, we were sitting on a little couch on one side of the office. I hadn't noticed it when I came in, cannot recall how we wound up sitting there. We faced each other and her knee (demurely cloaked in the long, blue skirt) remained lightly pressed against mine. It was enough contact, again, like

I was in junior high school, to keep the hard-on raging. I couldn't think of anything other than crushing my naked flesh against hers. A glorious picture filled my mind of lying back on her great mahogany desk while she impaled herself on me.

Finally, I shifted a little on the couch so that our knees no longer touched. The monkey cells cried out for contact again, their tiny voices dying away in my head as if they were actually dying. I wondered if I was losing my mind.

I finally got a hold of myself and looked at her.

Cat was wearing some kind of old-fashioned mascara that had run in great black gouts down her face as she cried, and insanely, I was reminded for a second of Alice Cooper. Then she took my hands and I leapt up – I felt that electric sex shock run through me again. What the hell was wrong with me?

I looked down at her raccoon eyes and reminded myself again who she was. The only one who'd gotten out of there alive (except for Sammy Mellucci, and like poor, young Scott Holland, could you call that living?)

I asked her again what happened.

Cat's voice was calm and low, with only an occasional sob thrown in to indicate the gravity of the tale. She asked me to sit. I told her I'd rather stand.

"I don't remember anything, Si," she said simply. "The last thing I remember is that day we all played dress-up."

"Are you saying that you don't know what happened?" I asked incredulously. I wanted to scream, *You called me!* I prepared to rail and accuse, to ask her why she'd burst into tears when she saw me, if she didn't remember . . .

But then she said, "Oh, yeah, Si, I *know*. I don't remember, but I *know*."

Cat arose and I involuntarily stepped back, not wanting her to touch me again. *Maybe later,* a monkey chittered in my brain. *Oh, most definitely, I'll want her to touch me later,* he said, *but not just right now.*

She didn't attempt to touch me, but went and sat down again behind her desk. She sniffled a little bit, and swiped at her eyes a little bit. She opened a drawer, and I noticed that it was one of those with the files in there sideways. Girlishly short, girlishly pink fingernails walked across the files, and I imagined them walking across my belly. I shivered.

Cat selected a file, not thick. She withdrew it from the drawer. "I wound up at State." The psychiatric facility, where Sammy Mellucci was now, still, if he hadn't died. "Apparently, I'd been walking around it the streets, not knowing my name."

"You had amnesia?" I said, feeling like a not too well-drawn out character in a bad cop drama. Despite what TV tells us, amnesia in healthy twenty-six-year-old women is just not a common occurrence.

Cat handed me the file and said, "Apparently, I started out at a homeless shelter, was there for a month or so, just following some old woman named Marty around, doing what she told me – stand here, sit there. Then Marty had a heart attack or a stroke or something, and since I was practically catatonic, they sent me to State."

I thought that it could be more shoddy police work, or it could be that she was lying through her teeth. Solly and I had sent her picture to every homeless shelter and mental hospital in three counties. Funny how she hadn't turned up.

"Eventually, after about six months in the hospital, I started to remember who I was," Cat said. "I asked why no one had come to see me." The tears began to leak from the big browns again, causing new black freshets to slide down her cheeks. "I asked why my friend Sandy hadn't come to see me. Dr. Sanborn looked Sandy's name up. He told me that she was dead." The sobs now, and more tears. "He thought that maybe her death had somehow triggered my amnesia. When he thought I was ready, he showed me the newspaper clipping."

Cat gestured at the file. I didn't have to look. I remembered it: *Nine Die in Drug Shooting.* It listed all the dead except for Billy, as her important daddy had kept her name out of the paper. The article said that police suspected that the massacre was the result of some kind of drug deal gone awry, that the ladies and gentlemen had been at the wrong place at the wrong time. Caught between possibly gang-related crossfire.

It was all bullshit; we suspected no such thing. There were no drugs. Nobody was even *on* drugs. And as you know, gentle listener, no one was shot.

"So you think Sandy was shot?" I asked Cat now. "Over drugs?"

"I don't know anything but what I read in the paper," she replied. "The doctor said my friends were dead, and showed me their names in the paper. He asked me if I thought that this, *this incident,* might've been shock enough to send me into amnesia."

I still held the folder, unopened. I asked her, "And what did you say?"

Now she favored me with an angry, smoky glare. "I told him that the last thing I remembered was that day when we all played dress-up. I told him that yes, finding out that all my friends were dead might indeed have sent me over the edge."

I asked, "And then what happened?"

Cat shrugged. "They gave me some tests, decided that I'd sufficiently regained my faculties, and sent me home."

I was appalled. "No one at the hospital called the cops?"

Cat shrugged again, and somehow, it was like a jaguar shivering. "The doctor said that he'd spoken to the police. He told me that they said that the case was closed."

"*Closed?* It isn't closed!" I told her. "And you never went in yourself? You could've been a material witness, for Christ's sake, Cat! Maybe you were there when it happened, maybe you saw it – and that's what gave you amnesia. Maybe they could've hypnotized it out of you. Maybe they could still hypnotize it out of you."

The *maybe you did it* remained unsaid.

Again, the smoky, angry glare – then it softened and the tears welled up again. "I was scared, Si! I couldn't've been there, or the drug dealers would've shot me too, wouldn't they? I didn't remember anything. How could I help the police, if I didn't remember anything?

"I didn't want anyone to hypnotize me, to *make me* remember. I just wanted it all to stay forgotten. So I left town, went to school. I met a wonderful woman; she gave me a job here." Cat sighed, a little hitch catching in her throat. Then she said, "Will you pardon me while I wash my face?"

I nodded, and she disappeared behind a door. I heard the water running.

It was all too pat. Amnesia. Right. Even this little intermission, so she could wash her face and I could peruse the file that she'd shoved at me.

Well, I'm a good boy, a good monkey – so I opened the file and pawed through it. Xeroxed documents reflected the paper trail of the story that she'd told me – admission record of a Jane Doe to State, with her picture, looking blank and stupid; doctor's notes and recommendations, release record from State, and of course, the *deus ex machina* – a copy of that newspaper clipping that supposedly explained everything.

Again I felt like a character in a bad cop show, or perhaps a print murder mystery this time, since all the paperwork was so in order. All of this could've been faked, of course. And even after eighteen years, all of it could be checked. There was no statute of limitations on murder, even though I knew it would probably be impossible to pin any of this on her now – especially since the only corroborating witness, Sammy Mellucci, if he'd ever been competent to testify, he surely wouldn't be any more, not after eighteen years in the laughing college.

I imagined that I could still rattle Cat's cage about it, though, make life a little uncomfortable for her for a few weeks while we ran a little investigation. It would be quite the embarrassment to her, I thought, to have some flat foot walking around here interviewing all the debutantes. And their rich parents.

She couldn't've been at any homeless shelters, I thought again, couldn't've been at State. Solly and I had sent out pictures – there'd been an APB. Her story was bullshit.

Cat emerged from her executive's washroom precisely on cue. She looked at me evenly, and again I felt a stirring in my loins, as it were, so immediate and profound that I had to look away. What was wrong with me? Where was this coming from? Cat was the enemy, here. I believed that she knew why what happened to Sandy had happened. I believed she might even know who did it.

After a heartbeat, I looked back at her. She'd not reapplied her makeup; she'd simply wiped it all off. *Perhaps she felt more tears might be in the offing,* I thought. I knew Cat couldn't be a day under forty-four, because we'd all been about twenty-six when the tragedy had occurred, and that'd been eighteen years ago. But I asked myself now, even without any makeup – or, *especially without any makeup* – if I didn't know that Cat was forty-four, and somebody had told me that she was thirty-two, would I for one second have doubted it?

At last she spoke. "But you aren't here about what happened to Sandy."

I flinched when she used the exact same expression that I always did. *What happened to Sandy.*

"No," I replied. "I'm here about what happened to Carly Dutch."

"Of course." Cat nodded and sat down behind her desk again. "I've already spoken to the police." She glanced at her computer again – apparently her day planner was on the screen, because she asked, "Who is Detective Solomon Nova? It says here that I had an appointment with him." She looked at me evenly again. "No one said anything about *you.*"

I said, "That's my partner. He was unable to attend today, so here I am."

Cat gestured at a chair in front of her desk, where I would've been sitting all along, if it hadn't been for the sobs and the hugs and the hard-ons and the knees pressed against me on the sofa, and the walk down a blood-spattered memory lane, and her lies and after-the-fact alibis.

I sat in the chair and she said, "What more do you want to know about Carly, Si? What more can I tell you, that I haven't already said to the other policemen?"

I handed her file back to her, desperately wishing that I had one of my own to flip through, one that concerned Carly Dutch. But Sol had the file. "My partner and I, we were just assigned to this case," I lied, "so we're playing a little catch-up. Did you know Carly personally?"

Cat smiled and again a shiver dove down my back.

"I've known Carly all her life, Si. I brought her birth mother and her adoptive mother together. We were all sorority sisters."

And then she proceeded to tell me the heartwarming story of a sorority sister in trouble and a young Mrs. Dutch. Mrs. Dutch – having already graduated, married, and given birth, had been left tragically barren after Jonathan's arrival – and she just happened to be visiting her own sister at the sorority house. She'd been reminiscing with sis about her glory days there at Kappa Kappa Whatever, when Cat had brought the other one, the one in trouble, and Mrs. Dutch together.

Appropriate gestational months later, Carly had been born, the Dutches had adopted her, all above-board, all legally. Everyone had more or less lived happily ever after, until this recent alleged castration incident, and Carly's subsequent disappearance.

Except – Cat squeezed out another tear – the sorority sister in trouble had died in a car accident shortly before graduation. *How convenient,* I thought, and half expected Cat to present me with another file full of adoption records and death certificates.

"Of course," Cat said, "Carly doesn't know that I knew her biological mother. Or that I have anything more than just a passing acquaintance with her adoptive mother. And I don't, really. It's not like we socialize."

I tried to return her level stare, but found it difficult. "Has Carly shown up here since the incident?"

"Not to my knowledge, Si." Cat smiled then, and to my dismay, I found that looking at her smiling mouth caused another almost immediate erection. "And not much that happens here escapes my knowledge."

The intercom buzzed, and Cat looked away from me to answer it. The secretary apologized for the interruption, but said that the urgent call from out of town that Miss Catarina had been waiting been for was now holding on Line One. Cat said, "Tell him that I'll be right with him."

Again she looked directly at me, and again I felt that sex-electric skewering through the balls. "I'm sorry, Si, but I have to take this. Would it be too much trouble to ask you to come back later? Would you come by my house tonight?"

I stammered, "That really won't be necessary, Cat – I have to talk to my partner. I really don't have any more questions for you about this right now."

I really didn't. Anything that I wanted to ask her now, to tell her, to say to her at all, surely didn't have anything to do with any type of police work. Not anymore. The only thing that I wanted to tell her now was what I wanted to do to her. And I'd really just as soon show her as tell her.

"I'd just like to see you again, Si," Cat was saying. "It's been too long." She produced a piece of paper from another drawer and slid it across the desk to me. It was a map of the campus with the *Director's Residence* already highlighted.

Cat said, "Can you come back tonight? I've missed you, Si. I'll cook dinner for you. Say eight o'clock?"

Before I could gather the power of speech to demur, I had a dinner date with Miss Catarina, the Director of the exclusive Zagairre School. With my dead wife's one-time lesbian best-buddy, Cat Miner. With the enemy. With the sexiest woman I'd seen in a long time. *A very long time*, apparently, considering my reaction to her.

I nodded, because the power of speech had not yet returned.

"I'll see you then, Si," she said, and when I didn't stand up to leave fast enough, she added, "I really have to take this call."

Again, I nodded like a mute. I finally stood up and got the hell out of there.

I welcomed the inside of the government-issue Ford, as if it was some kind of sanctuary. I'd taken the stairs down from the Director's Office two at a time, like the demons of the pit were after me. I sat in the car and panted, and it wasn't entirely as a result of the exertion of my flight.

The hard-on was just then fading, and again I wondered just what the hell was wrong with me. Sure, I'd always thought Cat was cute, but never would I have believed that seeing her again would elicit this kind of response from me. I believed that she'd probably had something to do with Sandy's murder, and I believed that regardless of the depth of her involvement in *that,* she was undoubtedly just as crazy as a shithouse rat. And these beliefs hadn't changed, no matter how dressed up she was, nor how young she looked.

I remembered that time that she'd grabbed my crotch, with Sandy just in the other room. I'd found that little act a bit overbearing at the time, not much of a turn-on. But at that time, there'd been no other woman for me but Sandy, so the gesture had struck me as annoying instead of alluring.

Now, Sandy was long gone. Still, I couldn't figure out where this sudden rush of lust had come from. It wasn't like Cat had grabbed me by the dick and bit my ear *this* time. She hadn't made one flirtatious remark, overtly or otherwise.

I shook my head and started the car, simultaneously pushing the button that summoned Sol on my phone. I thought that perhaps God's gift to women might have some kind of professional insight into the reason why I'd suddenly, *literally,* developed a hard-on for the enemy.

But Solly was rushed, non-committal. "Oh yeah?" was all he'd say. He told me that he'd called in sick after his little fender-bender that morning. He said that he'd catch me later – he was in the middle of something right then, okay? *I just met this chick, gotta go, will explain it all later, you won't believe it, gotta go, talk to you in the morning, bye.*

I threw the phone at the passenger seat, a favorite action when I was angry at whoever had been on the other end. But was I really mad at Sol, or just myself?

Or was it more like disgust? The memory of embracing Cat, of how her body molded to mine, was like a burr between the folds of my brain, a pleasant irritant that I couldn't seem to shake. There was a ringing in my ears, a fire in my blood – all the tiresome clichés fit. I realized in astonishment that I wanted Cat like I'd never wanted any other woman in my entire life.

What's that you say? Not even Sandy? Oh, yeah, I wanted Cat *way* more than I'd ever wanted Sandy. This desire was a selfish thing, a *me thing*. I wanted Cat for me, for my own satisfaction, for my own release, *right now*.

Sandy had been the once-in-a-lifetime love of my life, and my desire for her had been tempered by that love. Does that make any sense? There'd been love for Sandy, and affection for Sandy, and also desire for Sandy. She was my friend, as well as my wife, my lover.

But there was only desire for Cat, welling up from some black cave within me. I didn't love her – I didn't even particularly *like* her. She was the distrusted enemy. At worst, she was maybe a mass murderer; at best, she was definitely a liar.

But all that didn't keep me from wanting, *needing,* to fuck her brains out at the first available opportunity. It was a visceral, animal thing – not at all a pretty sentiment.

Driving back to the office, I mused over the nature of fear and lust and how it must affect men and women differently. They say that women have rape fantasies – I've seen the aftermath of a few rapes, and I doubt if any of *those* women had any rape fantasies. I doubted if normal, self-respecting women could really want to do someone that they were truly afraid of. I couldn't imagine how any woman could put herself in such a vulnerable position, if she knew that there could be the possibility that this stronger other could hurt her in the middle of it.

On the other hand, what I knew about women wouldn't fill a match book.

But with men, it's all different, I know that much. Normal, self-respecting men are just not afraid of something that they want to fuck, even if they should be.

Here was a perfect example. Miss Catarina had been accused by a half-castrated bad-ass of being the castrator. Even if the method he'd described was just crazy, Sammy had tapped her picture and said, "Yeah, that's her." In law enforcement, we call that a *positive identification.*

I was only here at Zagairre School because I suspected that the massacre of missing dicks and ice picks and robot chicks might somehow be connected to the loss of poor ol' Scott Holland's little friend, at the hands of one of the younger members of the student body.

And now it turned out that Cat, the original castration suspect, knew Carly, the new, accused castration suspect. Cat had known Carly from before she was even born.

Any thinking, red-blooded American man in my shoes would be afraid, right? I should've been shopping for cast iron underwear, right?

But not me. Not only was I not afraid, I wanted to go right ahead and stick my head in the lion's mouth, did I not? I certainly wanted to stick something somewhere, and was single-minded in my desire. Common sense, or anything as ridiculous as an intelligent sense of fear, wouldn't stand in my way.

The fact that I was thinking about how crazy I was indicated that I did have some intellect left, some sense of self-preservation. But the fact that I had absolutely no intention of failing to show up at the *Director's Residence* at precisely eight o'clock and giving the Director every inch of whatever she asked for, proved that, for the most part, the monkeys were in charge. It proved that, even at forty-four, your basic human male can be persuaded quite easily to stop doing the important thinking with the head between his shoulders.

All the way back to the office, is was like this – back and forth in my mind. But it was not the angel and the devil perched on my shoulders, arguing for my soul. This wasn't a question of right versus wrong. Sandy was dead; if she was in some afterlife looking down on me, I knew she wouldn't object to my fulfilling a basic human need, especially one that'd so suddenly and brilliantly flared to life.

No, this wasn't a question of right versus wrong – this was a question of smart versus not smart. My dick sat on one shoulder, repeating, "Just do it!" My brain sat on the other shoulder, urging me to remember that this woman that I suddenly wanted to fuck so very badly was a suspect in one helluva a bunch of death and mutilation, and a suspected accessory to more mutilation.

Solly had left the brochure from Zagairre on the dashboard, and that cruel, reptile aspect of my brain suggested that, hey, why don't we just swing by State and show that picture of Miss Catarina to Sammy Mellucci. Tell him that she was just down the road from him, calling herself the director of a school for rich girls, nowadays. My brain said that maybe I should judge how to handle this situation by gauging Sammy's reaction. Maybe I'd smarten up from watching him try to climb through the barred windows to get away.

I mediated these two opposing voices by stating to them, to myself, that I had not indeed lost my objectivity, or my caution – or least of all, my suspicion. I'd continue my investigation, and if I discovered that Miss Catarina was implicated in these events in any way, I'd send her right off to jail, just like Batman did to Catwoman. No matter how hard I fucked her first.

But that was just going to have to be the very next step.

Later that evening, on my way back to Zagairre for my dinner date with the Director, on my way to meet my fate, I spotted a Mexican kid selling bunches of flowers out of a white plastic bucket. He'd stationed himself at the bottom of the hill, before the long wooded road climbed up to the exclusive school. I figured if he'd gotten any closer, one of the guards would've been dispatched to roust him. Couldn't have that kind of riff-raff hanging around.

So I bought a bouquet for Cat, trying to prove to myself that there yet existed inside me some ghost of the romantic.

But just before turning onto the grounds, I glanced over at the flowers. They were carnations, white flecked with red, and suddenly I was reminded of the cheap nylon nurse costume Sandy had been wearing when she'd been butchered, her red blood seeping up the white material like licking flames, her white stockings and shoes flecked with red gore.

I threw the bouquet of carnations out the window.

But did this sudden wave of disgust and despair stop me in my single-minded monkey pursuit? It most certainly did not. It didn't even prompt a pause.

The front of the *Director's Residence* looked like a little cottage from a gardening magazine, with flower-lined, stepping-stone path and half-timber façade. Large trees disguised the fact that it was actually a roomy, comfortable, newly constructed two-story house.

I rang the doorbell. Cat opened the door. She smiled. I smiled and stepped inside. She closed the door. We looked at each other, and I opened my mouth to say some greeting, some pleasantry, but the look on her face silenced me. No words were necessary, as language is, of course, a tool of the higher brain. The monkeys screamed in my head and I grabbed her, and we coupled right there on the foyer floor, in front of the closed – but not locked – front door.

Afterward, Cat threw her clothes quickly back on, so I did the same, everything but my jacket and my gun, which I left draped over a chair. She brought out dinner, and *now* she became talky, prattling on about the Dutch girl, how she'd watched little Carly's progress since the seventh grade, and what a shame it was that all this had happened. Mostly, Cat stressed that she couldn't imagine where the little girl had gotten to. She hoped that Carly had found some friend to take her in, but then thought again that that was probably doubtful, as Carly's picture had been all over the news, and no parent would've been so irresponsible as to shelter her after seeing that.

I said little. I just let her blather on, enjoying the delicious Italian meal that she'd whipped up, wondering vaguely if she'd really cooked it herself, or if maybe there was a staff somewhere that had achieved it for her.

Eventually, what was passing for conversation – but was really just Cat's protestations of ignorance – petered out. When silence at last fell completely, I looked up from my spumoni to find her gazing hungrily at me again. She arose and came around the table, and whispered in my ear, "Do you have any handcuffs, Si?"

Surprised, but somehow not surprised at all, I smiled at her and replied, "As a matter of fact, I do, Cat. They're in the car."

She gathered up my ice cream bowl and spoon, letting me think about it for a second while she carried them out to the kitchen. Then she returned and said, "Why don't you go get them and meet me upstairs?"

I nodded, a stupid grin pasted on my face. You didn't have to tell me twice. I skipped out to the car and retrieved a pair of handcuffs from the trunk, a special pair that Solly had given me for just this kind of thing.

I went back into the house and retrieved my gun and its holster from the chair where I'd left them, then sprinted up the stairs to her bedroom, feeling like a man half my age.

Another fleeting flash of self-loathing – how *could* I be doing this when I didn't trust this woman still, when I still didn't even like her? I answered myself that it was obvious that she more than a little bit liked me, and, who knows what might be gleaned from a little pillow talk?

Besides, I just couldn't help myself.

When I got to her room, I found that it was all done in shades of pink and I felt a little stab of guilt, thinking of Carly Dutch, still missing. I told myself that perhaps this was not, after all, the most conscientious way of going about this investigation. But, as I've mentioned, my mind wasn't in charge. It'd started to come back a little bit during dinner, but once Cat had started looking at me and asking about handcuffs, it was pushed out again, with only these feeble flashes of sanity to remind me that I was anything more than just a dick with legs.

I heard water running, and set my gun in its holster, the handcuffs, and their key on the bedside table. I peeped into the open door of the bathroom. Cat was seated in a huge, round, whirlpool bathtub, and she beckoned me in. I retreated to the bedroom, disrobed, and returned to her.

The blank mammal intensity was the same as earlier, if not more so. At one point, I think I lost consciousness, and only slipping under the hot, bubbling water revived me. It was incredible.

Then she was climbing out of the tub, again beckoning, her naked twenty-five-year-old's body glistening and impossibly perfect. I followed, then she turned and pushed me backwards onto the bed. She grabbed my right wrist, and I dutifully allowed her to handcuff me to the impressive brasswork of the headboard.

She saw the gun on the night table, and pouting prettily, she said, "Were you planning to shoot me, Si?"

I didn't feel that it was necessary to explain to her that I was a cop and I always kept my piece where I could reach it. This was the major duty and major benefit of being a cop. A regular guy who keeps a gun within sight is a paranoid nut; a cop that does so is just a cop. Even a good cop. Isn't that what TV has taught us?

But to make Cat feel safe, to show her how much I trusted her, I reached across with my left hand and demonstrated that, handcuffed to the bed, I couldn't reach the weapon, even if I did decide that she needed to be shot.

This satisfied her. She climbed astride me and I wouldn't't've believed that I could rise to the occasion again – what was this, the third or fourth time tonight? But there was nothing else to do, she was that incredible. I think I could've exhibited superhuman powers of tumescence at her whim. Seek medical attention for an erection lasting more than four hours, unless it's some insatiable redhead commanding it. I think I could've continued like a jackrabbit, until I fell over dead from exhaustion.

But, alas, that was not to be. This would be our last time. After I was through, she waited a polite interval, then slid off of me. She ignored the handcuff key on the night stand as she arose, then glided to the bathroom and returned wearing a black silk robe with a green dragon on it.

I was thinking about how clichéd that was – again, like bad porn – when she sat down on the bed beside me and began to speak.

"I've got an incredible story to tell you, Si. Will you sit there like a good, little, naked handcuffed boy and listen to my story?"

Quick as lightning, Cat grabbed my arm and jerked it up and then downward, slamming the cuff painfully into the bones around my hand, making quite sure it was still secure.

She smiled and said, "It looks like you have no choice."

Then she waited for me to say something. I sensed a change in the mood and remained silent.

When I just looked at her evenly, Cat began again. "This is an exceedingly strange and bizarre story, Si, and I don't expect you to believe it as I'm telling it to you. But, by the time I get to the end, I expect you'll believe it. I expect you'll have no choice but to believe it, strange as it is, because it'll explain so many things.

"And while I'm telling you this story, Si, you'll wonder *why* I'm telling you. I bet you'll wonder that more than once. And the reason is simple: I'm hosting the biggest, most important gathering of my life in a few days, and I simply cannot have you and your little policemen friends running around asking unanswerable questions while these people are here at my school. It simply will not do. So, here goes.

"First, I want you to imagine another planet, Si, a planet similar to this one. But not entirely the same, you see? Similar, but not the same."

I laughed and told her, "I think I've heard this story already, Cat. Is this planet called Sirius?"

She blinked. "Sirius?"

"Yeah," I said. "Every alien story ever told starts with Sirius."

She blinked again. "No. The planet I'm talking about isn't Sirius, not even anywhere near there. The planet I'm talking about is called . . . Well, just never you mind what the planet I'm talking about is called. But it's most assuredly not Sirius. Sirius is . . . *problematic*. I've been told that they eat their enemies on Sirius."

I didn't know what she expected me to say to that. *Was this some kind of new sex game?* I wondered. The painful yank on my arm to make sure that I was unable to get away would seem to indicate that it wasn't, but who knew? She'd requested the handcuffs. Maybe I was going to be the trapped spaceman and she was going to be the devouring alien.

I remembered a time when Cat had looked at me like she wanted to eat me. Like with a knife and fork. Whatever. I just remained silent.

She continued. "This planet that I'm going to tell you about – this planet evolved, just like ours did, just like Sirius did. Eventually, a race climbed to the top of the food chain, and started a civilization there, just like we did here. They're similar to us, and their civilization is similar to ours, but not the same. It's important that you understand that, Si.

"Their civilization grew and their art and their science and industry flourished. In fact, these, these . . . For lack of a better word, let's just call them *people*. These people far outstripped us in science, energy, technology."

Cat arose and began to pace back and forth at the foot of the bed. "Perhaps, before I describe all their great technological advances, I should first underline the structural differences between our species. Because in the end, this explanation will provide all the answers – it is these differences that really make all the difference." Cat blinked at her own stupid, childish turn of phrase.

I still said nothing.

She began again. "Now you're going to have to use your imagination a little bit, here, Si, because some of the things I'm going to describe next are literally out of this world."

I thought that Cat had no idea of the depth and breadth of my imagination. She wanted to describe aliens? I could imagine aliens with no problem whatsoever. I'd imagined aliens out of meteorites, once upon a time.

"Are you familiar with the concept of sexual dimorphism, Si?" Cat asked, and then didn't wait for me to reply, but immediately explained it to me. I was just a dumb cop, after all, just a dumb cop who'd allowed himself to be handcuffed and now had to suffer all these explanations.

"Sexual dimorphism concerns the differences that allow one to distinguish between the genders. Sometimes it's ornamentation, like how female pheasants and peacocks and ducks are plain, while the males are flashy and brightly colored. Sometimes, it's a small difference in size, like with people – men are larger, women smaller. Sometimes it's an enormous difference in size – there are these spiders, where the male is tiny and the female is huge. Sometimes, the differences are even more pronounced than that – there is a kind of moth in Europe with the fanciful name of *Scarce Vapourer,* where the male has wings. He looks just like a regular moth. But the female is completely wingless.

"On this other planet, as I've said, there arose a race of people, just like here on Mother Earth. They even resembled us, in many aspects. Their build is about the same, as far as height and weight are concerned. The amount and location of body hair is the same. The hands, arms, shoulders, back are all the same, though their fingers are just a tad longer than ours. Not long enough to notice a difference, really, unless someone pointed it out to you. Legs and feet are identical.

"The female carries the fetus within her body, and suckles him at two breasts, located in the same place as ours. Skin and eye color vary, just like with humanity. So, all in all, as far as body size and limbs and racial coloring, the people from this planet look almost exactly like us.

"But then the sexual dimorphism comes in. The differences between their men and women are rather more pronounced than the differences between our men and women. And the differences between us and them, *as a species,* involve the structures and the placement of the external sexual organs and the method of fertilization.

"The gonads of the males are in about the same place as on human men, however, there is no structure approximating a penis, at least not in that vicinity. Urination is accomplished through a small urethral opening not unlike that possessed by human women, as well as the women of their own species."

I must've looked dumbfounded at this fairy tale that Cat was weaving, because she stopped pacing and spelled it out for me. "The males have balls between their legs, but no dicks there. Do you get it?"

I nodded, and once more she began to pace back and forth across the room. Once more she assumed her scholarly inflection. "Instead of between their legs, the males on this planet have a penis-like appendage on their faces, in approximately the same place as our noses, although it serves no purpose in respiration, and none in actual fertilization, as I will explain momentarily. The eyes are located where our eyes are, and the nostrils are located between them, above the penis-like structure. The mouth is below it, hair on the top and back of the head, et cetera. I understand that the males look a lot like human men, actually."

I smiled to myself, but didn't actually smile, instead keeping an outward expression of intrigued interest. I imagined again that this really must be the beginning of some kinky sex game – Cat all teacher-like, instructing her captive student all about these guys with dicks on their faces. Yeah, they looked just like human men, if human men had their nostrils between their eyebrows, and squatted to pee like a woman – and of course, if we had our dicks on our faces. I couldn't wait to see what kind of role-playing this was going to devolve into.

Cat continued. "The females of this species, as has been mentioned, are also remarkably like human women, with the following major differences. Their eyes are in the same places as ours, however, they don't possess noses, only nostrils, which are located between their eyes, like their men. Starting from about where the bridge of our noses are, and completely hiding the mouth opening and the bottom half of the face, the females have prehensile tentacles of various lengths and thicknesses."

Suddenly, my amused, this-is-just-some-kind-of-kinky-sex-game inner-monologue evaporated. Cat was describing Sammy Mellucci's Cthulhu women.

She went on. "As I've said, the females have breasts like human women, and broad hips for childbearing, like us. They're curvy." She described a womanly shape in the air with her hands. "The external vaginal and urethral structures are similar, as are the internal uterine structures. Other internal reproductive structures differ vastly, however."

Cat stopped pacing and looked at me to make sure I was still paying attention. How could I not be paying attention? I was handcuffed to the bed.

"Are you following me, here, Si?" she asked. "This next part is very important."

I nodded, presenting the same expression I'd all along presented to her, that of intrigued interest. But I really was hanging on her every word now, ever since she'd mentioned Sammy's octopus-faced women. Now I thought that this crazy, rambling, sci-fi story might somehow actually get back to how my wife got killed, now that we were getting to the important part.

Cat continued. "It's perhaps easier to explain the differences between human females and these other-worldly females in the context of the reproductive act."

Insanely, the thought ran through my head – *is that what the kids are calling it these days? The reproductive act?*

"The male and female embrace, usually standing up, but not always," Cat said. "But they are always face to face. The member on the male's face becomes engorged, similar to a human man's reproductive organ. The female wraps her tentacles around it, drawing it into her mouth. She has glands that are stimulated by its presence there – located in about the same place as our tonsils. She also wraps her tentacles around the male's head. The male cannot, at this point, very easily break the embrace.

"Now, another tentacle-like structure emerges from the female's vaginal canal. This one has a retractable serrated edge. The serrated edge, equipped with an anesthetic, wraps around the males testicles and slices them off. He doesn't even feel it. The tentacle-like structure, along with the testicles, is then withdrawn back into the female's body. She eventually releases the male's member from her mouth and tentacles, and the act is completed.

"Inside the female's body, the male's testicles are processed, absorbed. And she may or may not become pregnant. Just like with our own species, the reproductive act doesn't always take. The male's testicles will grow back in about a week, sometimes two. Soon after that, he is again fertile."

Cat looked at me, and I nodded. Here was an interstellar explanation for some aspects of the crime I was concerned about. Alien women had landed and taken the balls of all those unsuspecting tough guys in the warehouse. They even had the anesthetic that the M.E. had theorized about.

I tried to say, "What about –"

But Cat came over and put her girlish finger to my lips and shushed me. She said, "You'll understand everything by the time I'm finished, Si." She resumed pacing, and continued.

"In time, these creatures unlocked the secrets of interstellar flight – they laid bare all the innermost workings of biology and genetics." Cat paused to let me digest the awesomeness of the technological achievements of the dick-nosed men and the tentacle-faced women, then she sighed and said, "But while all this history marched on, there arose a dislike and a distrust between the sexes. Sure, the vast majority of them went about their daily lives as they always had, interacting, loving each other. They were a great deal like us – some were monogamous, mating for life; some were serially monogamous. There were cads and scoundrels and bitches and whores among them, just like us.

"But not long after their version of artificial insemination came into vogue – like our own rooms with cups and pornography, the testicles were harvested from the males without any attendant tentacle or mouth usage by a female – about this time, there began to arise a rather dystopian world view among the males of the intelligentsia. They began to feel that they were abused as a gender; that the very sex act was degrading to them."

I had to agree with the poor alien guys. How awful it must be to be de-balled every time you got laid, even if it was only temporary. Maybe that anesthetic stuff wasn't always so good, maybe. Maybe it hurt sometimes. Maybe the tentacle-mouth blow job wasn't always worth it.

I thought that I knew where all this craziness was heading. Cat believed that somehow *she* was one of these aliens, and it'd been her and other nutcases unknown who'd castrated those guys. Because she couldn't've done it all by herself. Sammy had said that there'd been at least three others.

And now, years later, maybe Cat had somehow convinced Carly Dutch that she was an alien, too. Maybe Cat had taught her how to do the slicing, like I'd always suspected.

But why had they killed Sandy and all the other women?

Cat was saying, "You may liken it a little to our own women's suffrage, these males' concept that they were being mistreated. And while women here have indeed come a long way, baby," here she winked at me, "a vast portion of the males on this planet went quite a long way further, segregating themselves from their women, actually immigrating to a different continent.

"So here was the situation on their world. Approximately half of the male population was still down to reproduce in the traditional way – females harvesting testicles, females becoming pregnant, testicles growing back, everyone happy.

"But many other males decided to go and live on their own continent, to eschew sex altogether.

"Now I don't want you to get the idea that there was any kind of political totalitarianism going on here, Si," Cat said.

I'd not been getting that idea at all. I fervently hoped that she wasn't going to now launch into a discussion of the politics of this mythical crazy place that she'd invented in her unstable mind, however. That might take all night. I flexed my handcuffed right hand to keep the blood flowing.

"Think of it this way," she said. "Italians live in Italy, but they're free to come and go as they please. The males that objected to the sex act lived on their own continent. They still traveled around the world, and women and families traveled to their continent as tourists. A small number of women even lived and worked there. Any man could come and live there if he wanted to follow their non-reproductive practices. Any of them could leave and go back to the real world anytime he wanted."

Cat paused and looked at me. I must've looked unsure to her, because she decided that further extrapolation on this part of the fairy tale was necessary. "Think of it this way. The place where these celibate men lived was like a monastery. They had women friends and women employees. But they didn't have sex with women, because sex with women led to the temporary loss of their testicles, which in their *religion,* to continue with the monastery analogy, they'd come to feel was inherently wrong." When I said nothing, she asked abruptly, "Do you have any questions so far, Si?"

I thought that if I was going to get any real information about the murders, it was vital to make Cat believe that I was interested, that I was buying this ridiculous yarn. So I quickly thought up a question. "How did they keep up the population on the male continent if there was no reproduction? Didn't they just start to die off and the population decline?"

Cat smiled at my apparently intelligent question. "They sponsored schools on the other continents to attract converts, just like Mormons or Scientologists or Moonies or any other cults here. They had no trouble keeping their populations not only stable, but ever growing. I guess it wasn't difficult to scare little virgin boys into giving up what they didn't yet know that they were missing. I'm sure that human men could make sex sound terrifying to our own little virgin boys here, if they chose to do so. If they described it right." Cat grinned that knife and fork grin at me again. "Don't you think so, Si?"

I nodded, thinking that the mothers of a thousand serial killers had done just that.

Cat said, "The more the intellect of this society expanded, the more the very idea of having their testicles harvested became odious and distasteful to a larger and larger portion of the men.

"Currently, just over fifty percent of the male population ascribes to this movement. At first blush, it seemed to be just some kind of a homosexual fad – the males do have mouths, after all, if not tentacles. Think of Fire Island or San Francisco, but on a continent-sized scale. But not all of the males that joined were homosexuals; in fact, most of them are not.

"It is in reality a deeply suicidal movement, Si," Cat told me emphatically. "Not only do these men refuse to have sex with their women, they believe to do so is *wrong*. They believe that the testicle harvesting nature of the act makes one gender superior and the other a helpless victim. These men not only believe that sex is wrong; they believe that *reproduction* is wrong. They believe that their race is flawed. They believe that it should be left to die out."

I raised my eyebrows. That did seem a little excessive. But on the other hand, maybe that anesthetic *wasn't* so effective. Maybe it did hurt. Maybe, like the emergence of Wolverine's talons, it hurt *every time*. Maybe it wasn't worth it to them to carry on as a species, to inflict all of that pain on sons yet ungotten and unborn.

Cat didn't continue, because she was waiting for some response from me. So I said, "So, what happened?"

She was still emphatic, still upset about the idiocy of these alien men. She said, "So here are half the men, keeping their fecundity to themselves. They are acolytes to a future of oblivion. The average Joe, I think, probably couldn't perceive that looming oblivion. After all, there was a continent full of them, with more and more arriving every day. In their selfishness, they couldn't see the end of their race – all they could see was the fact that they'd no longer have to personally undergo an act that they'd suddenly found to be degrading. There were plenty of other avenues to stimulation that didn't involve testicle harvesting.

"It was almost the same as if all the male black widows and praying mantises decided that they didn't want to get eaten after sex anymore and decided to leave town. Where would that leave all the lady black widows and the lady praying mantises? Where would that leave black widows and praying mantises as *species?*

"These men figured, let the other guys be degraded and propagate. They were free here in their own country – free from all responsibility to their own kind. They were devotees to a cause, a cause that they felt was more important than continuation of themselves.

"And the propaganda that kept them coming, the excuse that they cited to mothers and sisters and wives and girlfriends for joining this cult – it was a story about how the male brain trust of scientists was at that very moment working on asexual reproduction in the laboratory. Parthenogenesis, if you will."

Cat paused, then out of the blue, she asked me, "Do you remember the movie *Logan's Run,* Si?"

I shook my head, hoping this wasn't an important part, because I'd never heard of it.

She frowned at my cinematic ignorance, and then explained. "It's about this society, where everybody has to die when they reach thirty. The leaders have the general population convinced that they *don't die,* however – they have them convinced that they go to this place and are supposed to be *renewed.* Only no one ever sees these renewed people again. Some people don't believe that they'll be renewed, and they run on their last day, and others chase them and that is the plot of the movie.

"The celibate men on their continent were like the gullible citizens in *Logan's Run,* Si. They really believed that their species would be renewed – they really believed all this claptrap about the development of asexual reproduction in a laboratory. They really believed that their kind would continue, even if they never gave up their seed again to contribute to the process.

"But the women could see the handwriting on the wall. They saw the statistics. Birth rates were declining – more and more males were making the decision not to reproduce every year. And the women scientists, they knew that this story about asexual reproduction was just a pipe dream. Science fiction. They knew that plants and nematodes and aphids and Komodo Dragons can reproduce through parthenogenesis, but not people, not even aided by science.

"These female scientists saw the ultimate folly of their stupid, selfish men – they saw the push, like lemmings, to jump off the cliff into species annihilation."

Cat paused again. She'd gotten herself quite a bit angry at the stupidity of these alien men. Since I was a helpless human man, quite vulnerable, and I didn't want her to take out her anger on me, I asked quickly, "So what did the women do?"

Cat smiled, thrilled that I was so interested. "Genetic engineering. A little selective mixing of the species, across the void of space. This is where we come in, Si. Where humans, people come in."

This is where murder comes in, I thought. *This is where crazy and sharp steel intersect to create butchery and death and heartbreak.*

Cat said, "These female scientists – boy, were they sharp, Si. They know all about us here on Earth, you see. They know how our biology works, how our minds work.

"They know about these things the same way you know about Australia. Others have visited here, and the information about us is available – just like you know all about kangaroos and sheilas and *G'day, mate* and shrimp on the barbie, even though you've never been Down Under.

"So, those scientists sent a little unmanned probe our way, as the first step in their genetic engineering project. When I say unmanned, I don't mean untenanted, however.

"All those probes that we sent to Mars were unmanned. But they had a million different electronic gadgets and stuff on them, right? The equipment we sent on the Mars probes wouldn't seem alive to us, but to someone of less developed intellect . . . The probe that the women scientists sent out – it was full of electronic gizmos also. But alien ones. Ones that might seem to be actually alive to our *Cro-Magnon* sensibilities. You might not realize it, but you've seen their probe, Si."

I began to feel a little sick; some sort of nauseating déjà vu gripped me. I knew exactly what Cat was referring to – the thing was sitting in the back of a drawer in my desk at home, on top of Sandy's file. Yeah, I'd seen the alien probe, from the moment it had landed. I'd even gotten the feeling at the time that it *was* an alien probe.

Apparently Cat, in her utter insanity, had gotten the same impression from the meteorite that I had – but then she'd parlayed it into a full-blown alien invasion delusion, complete with accompanying murder and mayhem. Had it not turned into a bloodbath, it would've been almost funny – I'd had the same *illusion* as Cat, if not the same *delusion.*

"The rocks," I said. "You're talking about the meteorite and the rocks."

Cat smiled again. "Yes! You do remember! But it wasn't a meteorite, and they were most certainly *not* rocks. Each of those rocks, as you so preciously call them, was really a kind of an egg."

There – Cat had used the same word, the same idea that I'd originally formed – they were not rocks, but *eggs.*

She continued. "Inside of each egg was a little robot, of a sort. Each one, like our own Martian probes, was capable of communicating with the scientists back on the other planet, conveying important readings about its surroundings.

109

"I imagine that we can send messages to our probes, too. But I'm sure they're in computer language, very mechanical, very straightforward – move this tire, move this arm. But the little robots from that other planet? The women were in contact with them so much, in sync with them so thoroughly, that to the outside observer, they seemed sentient. After a while, they actually *became* sentient."

Cat stopped pacing. She said, "Are you comfortable, Si?" and approached the bed. She pulled on my handcuffed arm, but gently this time. "I'm sorry about having to restrain you like this, but it's kind of important that you hear my whole story. I couldn't have you freaking out and running off in the middle of it before you have a chance to understand everything." She kissed me on the forehead, then tenderly on the mouth.

Then she leapt back up and started pacing again. "Okay, where was I? Oh yeah. The robots. You remember when Sandy found the container and the robot eggs?"

I nodded. *I was there,* I thought.

Cat was saying, "Of course, none of us knew what those little eggs were then – none of us knew what they were capable of." She grinned. "Oh, those scientists! They had certainly read their interstellar studies. They knew exactly how our brains worked, our nervous systems!"

Cat stopped pacing abruptly, and looked at me. She said softly, "This is one of those parts that you might find hard to believe, Si."

Right. *Like the tentacle-faced women and celibate-by-choice dick-nosed guys weren't ridiculous enough,* I thought.

She began again. "Inside each little robot was a mechanical brain that sent out a signal. Two signals, actually. One of the signals went back across the vast reaches of space to the mother world. But the other signal was transmitted to the nearest human female brain. And whose brain do you think received that very first signal?"

I didn't hesitate. I said, "Sandy's." It was only logical in the context of what I'd heard so far. Cat's story was crazy, but not incohesive.

"That's right!" Cat said, and clapped her hands together in glee at my ability to ferret out the obvious. "And what did the little robot's signal tell Sandy to do? The first thing that it told Sandy to do was to insert it into herself, like a tampon."

Cat stopped pacing and looked closely at me. She wanted some kind of a reaction, and when I gave her none, she narrowed her eyes suspiciously and said, "What do you think of that, Si?"

It was really no more shocking or ridiculous than anything else in her shocking and ridiculous story. It was certainly no more shocking and ridiculous then five dead, castrated men and five dead, disemboweled women.

I said, "I'm reserving comment until you're finished, Cat. Isn't that what you want me to do?"

This seemed to mollify her, and she continued. "Sandy did what she was telepathically instructed to do. The little robot climbed into her body, acclimatizing itself, sinking little roots and holders slowly into her flesh, growing, assimilating, until it was in position for its further works. Sandy only felt that she was having an unusually bad period."

Again, I felt that sick déjà vu feeling, remembering how Sandy had remained in bed for four days, had taken a pain pill *and* a sleeping pill, immediately after we'd recovered that meteorite. Immediately after there were suddenly only five eggs instead of six.

Cat was saying, "Sandy had no memory of what the robot had told her to do, or even that there *was* a robot. The next thing that the robot told her to do was to call me. We'd only met once before, when I'd made a delivery to the Ranger Station. But the robot made Sandy remember me, brought me to the fore of her mind. It told her to find my card, give me a call. Invite me to lunch."

Now Cat came over and sat beside me on the bed. She smiled smokily again and whispered, "You remember how I used to have kind of a warm for you, Si?" She ran her hand down my chest, across my belly, caressed my naked thigh. "Kind of like I do now?"

111

Cat stopped touching me, which I was grateful for, and stood up again. She said, "Well, that didn't really compare to the warm I had for Sandy. I'd never realized that I was capable of having these feelings for another woman. I'd never suspected that I had these feelings for Sandy, and I never would've dreamed that she had such feelings for me. But then she gave me a robot, and it all became clear.

"Once I inserted it, oh, my God! My desire for Sandy erupted like a volcano! We suddenly couldn't get enough of each other."

I had to speak up now, because here was another explanation for all the weirdness, no matter how ridiculous. "So, you're saying that the robots made you and Sandy gay?"

Cat nodded. She said, "Of course, we had no memory of the robots, or of inserting them. It just seemed like all of a sudden we needed each other."

I wanted to ask Cat if Sandy had ever expressed any qualms about their instant lust for each other. I wanted to ask her if Sandy ever had any second thoughts about what their newfound love was doing to me. But if you start asking a crazy person rational questions about their craziness – well, that way lies your own madness.

Cat continued. "Then one day, our eggs told us that we needed to get four more women. Since Sandy and I'd already become lesbians, how easy was it for the two of us to attract four more women? Of course, we didn't know that the eggs were directing us. We didn't even know that there *were* any eggs. None of the others would *ever* know. And by the time I found about them . . . Well, I'll get to that in a minute.

"So Sandy and I lured in the butches. Corralled them. We took them up into the woods and gave them their eggs. Of course, none of us remembered that that was what'd happened. We just remembered going camping.

"But I'd remember, later. It would all come back to me. How we all stood naked around the fire, inserting the eggs into each other, like some kind of Wiccan ritual."

I interrupted. "Why the sudden change then, after that? Nobody was a lesbian in that warehouse."

Now Cat smiled at me. "Are you familiar with mimicry at all, Si? Mimicry and how it's used by parasites? There's this little thing – it's a flatworm. It lives inside songbirds. It doesn't kill them, but it lives in their stomachs, like a tapeworm. When the time comes, it releases its eggs, which wind up on the ground, if you get my meaning. Well, there are the eggs on the ground, and there is the bird, up in the sky. How do the worms get back up into the birds?

"The eggs are eaten by a snail, and they hatch inside the snail. Now they're inside the snail, moving around in him, in his little snail blood, in his tissue. But still, how do they get back up into the birds? The birds that these flatworms need to infect, they don't eat the snails they're infecting now. They don't eat snails at all. I ask you, Si! *How do the flatworms get back up into the birds?*"

I shook my head, a little alarmed at her vehemence.

Cat came close to me again and whispered, "I'll tell you how they get back into the birds, Si. It was for the same reason that all of a sudden, the robots turned us from lesbians to whores.

"The baby worms travel to the snail's eyes, and make them change color and dance around, in quite uncharacteristic ways for snails' eyes. This activity attracts those birds, who wouldn't otherwise have noticed the snails, *as they do not eat snails*. But these snails have now become irresistible to the birds, and they eat *these* snails. Eat 'em right on up. The baby worms are now back inside the birds and they grow and mature and mate and thereby is the cycle of life continued, world without end, amen.

"There's another little worm that lives in damp places or in the water as an adult, but as a baby, it's a parasite of grasshoppers. It lives in the grasshoppers' stomachs and absorbs what the grasshoppers eat, again, like a tapeworm. They are very efficient, Si – if the grasshopper gets eaten, they're able to wriggle out of the predator that ate him. But again, the question is – if the adult worms live in or around water, how do they get out of the grasshopper and into the water when it's time to become an adult? Grasshoppers aren't even remotely aquatic, right? So what does the worm do? It incites the grasshopper to commit suicide, to drown itself, like Ophelia, so it can be back in the water again."

Cat paused, and smiled seductively at me again. I think that despite all the craziness, I might've still been game at that point, had she worked on me a little bit. But it was not to be.

She said, "I have another parasite/mimicry example from the wonderful insect kingdom for you, Si. One that may be even more apropos. This tiny, little beetle larva gets together with a bunch of its fellows, and they form themselves into a big bug ball at the top of a plant. Then they proceed to give off the smell of this female solitary bee. Pretty soon, the male solitary bee shows up, attracted by the smell, and tries to fuck the ball of larvae, convinced as he is, that they're a female bee of his species. As he tries to perform this act, the little worms climb onto his legs and body. When he actually does find a female bee and has relations with her, the larvae climb off of him and onto her. He passes them on to her, just like a sexually transmitted disease. Then she takes them back to her nest, where they proceed to devour the baby bees.

"Then there's this rat parasite. *Toxoplasma gondii.* What it does is manipulate the rat's behavior, so that he's no longer afraid of cats. The parasite wants the rat to get eaten by the cat, you see, because it wants to get *inside* the cat. It can only reproduce sexually inside a cat. It can reproduce asexually in any warm blooded animal, but it can only combine its genes with other members of its species inside a cat, so inside a cat is the place to be.

"Now, you'll agree that rats have been around for a while, and they've developed certain behaviors to keep themselves alive, right? Not the least of which is to avoid cats. But this parasite, it turns all of the rat's caution, shall we say, into rashness. This parasite doesn't make the rat sick or make it run crazy in any other way. It alters only the specific behavior of avoiding cats.

"What the parasite does is this: when an infected male rat smells cat urine, the parasite makes him get all excited – his brain lights up the same way it does when he smells a female rat. He decides that this is something he wants to check out. They can't prove that the parasite makes the male rat want to actually go and *fuck* the cat – but they've proven that it definitely makes him less afraid; it totally makes him bypass his evolutionarily gained avoidance behaviors.

"And this isn't a creature, Si, with eyes and teeth or even a brain of its own. It's a *protozoan*. All these parasite/host interactions fall under a category referred to by scientists as a *manipulation hypothesis*. It posits that parasites can change how their hosts think, act, respond – strictly to the benefit of the parasite, always to the detriment of the host."

That's why they call them hosts, I thought, *and not buddies.*

Her tale had taken another weird tangent now. First it was aliens, now it was mimicry and parasites. But I didn't care about birds and grasshoppers and bees and rats. I wanted to hear more about the murders, so I said, "What does all this have to do with what happened to Sandy?"

Cat said, "Don't you see, Si! The women from that other planet used us just like these parasites! They needed to implant their robots in women. So how do women attract other women? They turned me and Sandy into lesbians to attract other women! Just like the flatworms making the snails attractive to birds!

"Then after we'd all been fitted with our robots, they don't need any more women. So we don't need to be attractive to women any more. So all the lesbianism just dried up.

"Now, the alien women, they need human men. So how do they attract men? First they made us lose our fear, just like the rats – we lost all fear that something bad might happen to us if we solicit strange men from off the internet. Like the grasshoppers, they made us do suicidally stupid things, all for their benefit. They made us forget all our fears. All our morality.

"But how do they get the men to try to fuck the ball of worms that is us? Why, the robots just get us to tart ourselves up and turn ourselves into whores. They sent out signals to our brains that made us think that all these things were good ideas, Si, the only things to do.

"But I think that I didn't change all the way, somewhere along the line. Because I still wanted Sandy a little bit; I think that I was a little hurt when she wasn't interested in me anymore. Besides that, overall, I felt odd about the whole thing. Later, I'd think that perhaps my robot was defective, that it hadn't turned the right switches on, or hadn't turned them on completely. But at the time, I just felt strange, like I was in some kind of nightmare. I think that's probably why I called you, Si. I wanted out of the nightmare."

I said, "Why did the aliens need human men, Cat?"

Again she smiled. "That's really the question, the crux, is it not? Why did they need human men? You saw what happened at the warehouse, and being a man, you want to know why it happened. Well, I'll tell you why it happened.

"The alien women were there on their planet, with all their men moving away and whining about how they're being mistreated, et cetera, et cetera, et cetera. So the women scientists decided that they'd do some genetic engineering, like I said.

"They'd forget about their own males – fuck 'em, they were all turning into pussies anyway, and that couldn't *possibly* be good for the species. The women decided that they'd forget about their own males, and even forget about their own selves, after a fashion. All for the continuation of the species. But to continue the species, in these dire times, they reasoned, they'd have to *change* the species. They cast around for ideas, read their interstellar travelogues. Finally they decided that they'd take a page from the Sirians' playbook – they'd take a little bit of humankind and combine it with themselves."

How had I known that the invasion was coming?

"So, what they did was this, Si," Cat said. "Those little robots that they sent blended into our human woman bodies,

116

but grew into mechanical versions of the aliens' anatomy. They created within us replicas of themselves, you see, metallic tentacles that slithered out and castrated the unsuspecting men that they'd made us lure to that warehouse. We didn't know anything like that was going to happen, of course.

"Making all the arrangements for it – that all just seemed to be a good idea time at the time. Maybe a little disjointed sometimes, but a good idea. The warehouse, the tables, the ads, those horrible costumes."

Despite her words, it seemed to me that some part of Cat knew that none of it had *ever* been a good idea, not now, and not even at the time. But she'd gone along with it all anyway, hadn't she?

Cat sighed and said, "So, it went down like this. Everyone was doing what they'd been programmed to do, screwing these men that'd answered the ads. But in the middle of it, my guy hesitated for some reason. He looked down and saw the tentacle. He freaked out and punched me, and I fell off the table. He jumped up and fled.

"Then *they* came. There were three of them. I felt drugged for some reason, plus there was the fact that this asshole I was with had just socked me, causing me to fall off the table. So I was in no shape to run, like he did. After a moment, I barely managed to stand up.

This metallic thing was hanging out of me, like a braided cable or a bungee cord – but that's not really accurate, either. I looked down at it and screamed, but it seemed to say to me, 'Ours got away, Cat.'

"I stopped screaming abruptly. I was completely gobsmacked that the thing could talk. I said, 'What's happening?'

"The thing hanging out of me said, 'I was designed to harvest testicles. But ours got away.'

"I looked up then and a woman was standing there, pointing a weapon at me. She was wearing a helmet, and the bottom of her face was a mass of tentacles. Somehow I knew that the woman and the thing inside me were in cahoots. I

117

screamed again, and begged my talking tentacle, 'Please, don't let her shoot me! I'll help you harvest whatever you want! Only please, don't let her shoot me!' The tentacle was prehensile, and it moved – it seemed to look toward the woman thing."

I couldn't help it – it was just all so insane. I said, "It had eyes?"

Cat said, "No, it doesn't have eyes. But it still seemed to look at her. Then she started to speak to me, and after a few sentences, I realized that she wasn't speaking like we do. I couldn't see her mouth anyway – it was under all those tentacles. Her voice was in my head. She said her name was *Freya*." Cat paused, then continued. "Actually, she didn't really say that her name was Freya, but it sounded something like that in my head, so that's what her name was always been to me."

Even with the ghost of Sandy's murder foremost in my mind, even with the handcuffs, even with the obviously unhinged nature of Cat's mind, still the whole story had become so hilariously funny, I almost laughed out loud. But I managed to keep it together enough to say, "What did her voice say to you?"

Cat replied, "Freya told me pretty much what I've told you about the conditions between the genders on her planet. In conclusion, she said, 'We've come here to improve our race. We've harvested the testicles of a cross-section of your males to further this goal. Unfortunately, due to anatomical anomalies, their other reproductive organ was also removed.'

"She gestured, and I staggered into one of bays and looked down at one of the men. In shock, I said, 'You realize that theirs don't grow back? None of it – not the testicles, not the penis – none of it grows back?'

"The woman-thing named Freya shrugged and told me, 'That's why we euthanized them.'

"I looked at my friends, each unconscious on her bed. Apparently, the testicle harvesting had knocked them out. I asked, 'What's going to happen to them?'

"Freya began to speak in my head again. 'These, your sisters, are to make the ultimate sacrifice for the furtherance of our race. But mourn not, as they'll live on in glory in our memories, as the original vessels of our combined species. Some of their material, what you call genes, will also live on.'

"I looked at her in disbelief, in fear. 'You're gonna kill them?' I asked.

"Freya said, 'Unfortunately, there is no other way. They're martyrs to a greater good. The creature that lives within each of them has served its purpose. Each has harvested precious alien tissue, every cell of which will be utilized to the shining future of our race.'

"She cocked her head and regarded me, then said, 'Every creature has served its purpose, except for yours. You and your creature have failed in the task.'

"The word she used wasn't exactly *creature,* but it wasn't *robot* either. It was an alien phrase, and it registered in my mind as something that was *alive.* When I looked confused, she gestured and I looked down, just in time to see the tentacle disappear inside of me.

"I felt another scream welling up, but I quelled it. 'Please don't kill me!' I begged. 'I'm sorry that I – it – *we* – failed. Maybe I can help you in some other way.'

"Freya said, 'We'll allow you to bear witness to the martyring of your sisters. Then we'll allow you to decide your own fate.'

"The three of them went to the first bay, where Patty was propped up on her cot. Freya said, 'Her creature has performed well. All of them have.' She gestured down the line of bays. Then she looked at me and said again, 'Except for yours.'

"She looked at Patty again. 'Now, they must come forth and be returned to our world, so that the glorious metamorphosis may begin! Creature! Come forth!'

"And one of the other tentacled women grabbed me, Si, because I started to scream, as thin, sharp metal fingers began to slowly – oh, my God, it was so slow! They slowly sliced through Patty's belly *from the inside out.* She convulsed, flopped around on the table, but mercifully, she didn't wake up."

I remembered Pat's body. Cat might say she didn't wake up, but when I saw her, her eyes were open. I'll never forget that faraway, lifeless gaze.

Cat was saying, "At last, the shiny metallic thing was free. It was about as big as a large fist. The tentacle appendage was wrapped around a box-like center. I imagined that's where the removed organs were – safely stored for the trip across the universe to a greater future than they ever would've known here. The little knife-like fingers that'd sliced through Patty's belly had flipped the thing over until it was standing on them like legs, standing on her belly. Dripping blood and tissue, it *jumped up* from Patty's filleted body into a container that one of the women held open for it.

"I thought that I must surely pass out, but then I realized that if I did, they'd do the same thing to me. So I decided right then and there what I had to do.

"'Please,' I said to Freya, 'please don't make me watch anymore. I've made my decision. I'll be your servant here – you can't walk among us, not with how you look.' All the tentacles bristled and waved at that remark. I said, "But I can. I'll do whatever you want. Only, please don't make me watch anymore.' I looked at poor, dead Patty.

"'Very well,' Freya's voice echoed in my head. 'Your human intelligence has saved your life. I never realized the value of a liaison, but you've shown me my error. With you in place here, our plans with take mere years instead of decades.'

"'Is there any way that you can take this thing out of me?' I dared to ask. 'Since it – we – failed at our task?'

"'The creature is part of you now. We can remove it from you now, no more than we could remove it from your sisters, and have you live. It's become a part of you, growing and twisting into your human womanhood.' Then there was a smile in the voice in my head. 'But you'll find that there are benefits to its presence. And we can communicate to you through it.'

"And then I woke up in State one day, and finally remembered who I was. All of the paperwork in that file? All of that's true, Si. I really did have amnesia, that you so pooh-poohed. I finally remembered who I was, but absolutely nothing about what'd happened, just like I told you. The eggs, the warehouse, the aliens. I remembered none of it. They told me that Sandy and everybody else was dead, then they let me out of the hospital. I even got my old job back – I worked for a florist, remember?"

I didn't remember, but I nodded anyway.

"I had a social worker for a few months; she helped me to adjust. I got a little apartment, started getting on with my life. I even thought about getting in touch with you. I was always very fond of you, Si." Cat walked over and kissed me again. "Everything was going along fine. I remembered nothing – no dreams, no flashbacks. Nothing.

"Then, on the anniversary of their deaths, it started. It started as a vivid sex dream. The particulars escape me – it might even've been about *you.*"

Cat smiled and I got the impression that she was *most definitely* lying this time. She hadn't been dreaming about me at all. *I bet you say that to all the guys dumb enough to let you handcuff them to the bed,* I thought.

Cat was saying, "Anyway, I had orgasm after orgasm in my sleep, until at last I woke up, smiling. Sometimes a good sex dream is better than actual sex, Si. Because a good sex dream is always good, whereas actual sex not always is." She winked at me.

"Then I heard a voice in my head. At first, I thought I was going crazy, like anyone would."

Again, I suppressed a sudden, entirely inappropriate desire to laugh. Anyone would think she was crazy, all right. Even before she mentioned hearing voices.

"But the voice explained to me, reminded me, made me remember. It told me that it was the creature inside of me. I quickly learned that I didn't have to talk out loud to it. I could just think my responses, and it would hear me.

"When I told it that I thought I was going crazy, that I thought I had to be imagining it, that I didn't believe there was really a creature living inside me, it demonstrated its presence by producing another one of those earthshaking orgasms. I said I still didn't believe in it, didn't believe that it was really there. It produced another orgasm. This went on for some time."

I'll just bet it did, I thought.

"At last, I realized that I couldn't be doing this all by myself, even if I *was* crazy. There had to be some kind of outside agent doing it." Cat winked at me again. 'Or in this case, *inside*."

"The thing continued to talk to me. It made me remember what'd happened to Sandy and the others. It reminded me of my promise to Freya, to be their liaison here on Earth.

"I was emboldened, because there were no tentacle-faced women around, waving weapons in my face. I said to the thing, 'What if I've changed my mind about all that?'

"And the thing said, 'I'd be very disappointed to hear that, Cat. Because if you've decided that you no longer want to cooperate, then Freya will undoubtedly call me forth, and you'll die. You know too much to be left alive, if you've decided to go back on your promise. If you've decided be her enemy.'

"I started to cry then, Si. Who wouldn't be afraid of such a threat? I knew I had no other choice but to cooperate."

Cat looked at me, her big brown eyes brimming with tears. I nodded sympathetically, all the time thinking that she was just as nutty as squirrel shit.

Somehow, she'd developed some kind of split personality. Maybe she'd always had one, who knows? Now she was going to start telling me about how this voice in her head started giving her orders. She was going to tell me about how she was compelled to do whatever the voice said, just like Norman Bates. Only the imaginary voice didn't come from Cat's mother, like Norman's did. Cat's imaginary voice came instead from the orgasm-producing, failed-at-testicle-harvesting, alien parasite that she believed lived inside her womb.

And they wonder why we drink, I thought. *Now, I've truly heard it all.*

"The thing comforted me," Cat was saying. "It revealed that I could have cosmic orgasms at my whim, with or without a partner, because they were brought on by the thing working inside me. It told me that I could have whatever body shape I desired, fat or thin, because it could monitor my metabolism and hormones to whatever end I desired. It said that it could even change my hair color for me – it was just a matter of turning around a couple of genes.

"And it told me that I'd age very, very slowly. That's why you see the same Cat before you today, Si, or maybe even a little better one, than the Cat you knew all those years ago." Cat dropped the robe off one shoulder and posed, smiled seductively. Then she winked at me and resumed pacing again.

"The thing advised me, Si – it told me what they wanted me to do with my life. It told me where they wanted me to go to school, what they wanted me to study. The people that I met, the movies that I saw, the classes that I took – the thing discussed them all with me. It told me how my destiny was being guided by the women on the other world.

"It didn't say this to me in a bossy way. After all, it said, the two of us were in this together. The alien women didn't really need it any more than they needed me, since we'd failed together in our initial harvesting attempt. After all, that's what it was – a mechanical testicle harvester, made after the structure in their own bodies. It hadn't been designed to linger inside for all this time, and it told me that if something happened to me, Freya and her minions wouldn't hesitate for a minute to destroy it. It wasn't like it was reusable.

"But the thing also told me that it liked me, that it liked being inside of me. That it'd grown to think of itself as more than just a harvester. That it thought of itself more as my friend.

"It explained to me that the alien women were very happy with my progress. When I asked what my progress was supposed to be toward, it told me about The Plan.

123

"The testicles and some genetic material from my martyred sisters had been taken back to their planet. They'd been doing some bioengineering with it. The goal was simple, Si. They'd create a new race that would bypass their men entirely. They wanted to die out? Let them. The Plan was to take some human stuff and combine it with their own to create a new woman. Not a new race, just a new woman. This woman would look like us: bye-bye tentacles." Cat put her hand under her chin and waved her fingers. "But the new woman they created would possess the actual tentacle harvesting equipment that they had. No more mechanical devices."

Cat paused to let that sink in. "The Plan consisted of three waves. The first wave had already been completed. That involved the creation and implantation of the mechanical harvesting devices in me and my friends. They were crude, single use. They killed their host after harvesting was completed. That part of the plan had been designed just like the plan for the dog that the Russians launched into space – they'd never intended for it to survive.

"The alien women were not insensitive to my friends' sacrifice, however. To honor them, some of their genetic material was included in the beings created in the second wave. My creature informed me that it couldn't help but be so, because the girls' genetic material was incorporated into the other creatures during their growing period, and it fairly clung to them when they emerged."

Cat paused, then began again. "When I was a senior in college, I rented an apartment with a girl named Victoria Robertson. She was younger than me, since I was a little late in starting my college career. I was thirty-one or so, and she was about twenty-three.

"One night, I woke up to find one of the alien women standing in my room. I cursed my thing for not telling me that she was coming. It was affronted at my rebuke, telling me churlishly that it hadn't been informed that the woman was coming.

"I couldn't tell if the alien woman before me was Freya from some years before, or someone new. They tend to look a lot alike. She gave me two vials. She telepathically instructed me to place the powder contained in one of the vials into some food and give it to Vicky the next evening. In the other vial was something that looked like a large bean. It was purple-black, the same color as the eggs that'd turned into the deadly robot-creatures. After I drugged Vicky and she passed out, I was supposed to drop the bean into her bed.

"I cried to the woman. I told her that I didn't want any more of my friends to die! The woman assured me that Vicky wouldn't die. She told me that the bean wouldn't grow into anything even remotely like the creature that lived inside me. The bean would grow into only a *temporary parasite,* she told me, and there was a laugh in her voice.

"Then her telepathic voice sobered. If I refused to comply, she said, then she'd simply call the creature inside me forth, and I'd die, and she'd carry out the work on Vicky anyway, without my help. Reluctantly, I agreed.

"The next night, I drugged Vicky, as instructed. She became sleepy while we were still sitting on the couch, watching a movie. She didn't even make it to her room, but passed out right there.

"I took the bean out of its vial. It was smooth and warm to the touch. I placed it on Vicky's knee and held my breath. After a moment, it broke open – for lack of a better word, let's say it *hatched* – and a metallic bug crawled out. It looked like a bug, anyway – like a large, shiny tick with lots of legs. It seemed to turn and look at me – but then again, it didn't really have a head – but still, it paused and seemed to raise a couple of legs in my direction, like it was thanking me for releasing it. Then it turned around and started slowly climbing up Vicky's thigh. I watched it for another minute – it moved very slowly – but then I couldn't stand it anymore and went out to the kitchen and made myself a sandwich. I stood in front of the sink and ate it, gazing blankly out the kitchen window at the street below.

"When I returned to the living room, Vicky was standing up, smiling. She stretched and said, 'Sorry I passed out on you, Cat. I must've needed the sleep. I just had the weirdest dream!' Vicky winked at me and I knew exactly what kind of a dream she'd had, what kind of a dream the little creature had produced for her. She smiled again and told me that she was going to go to her room and get in bed and try to have another dream just like that one.

"Three weeks later, Vicky came to me and tearfully confided that she was pregnant. I opened my mouth to tell her to get rid of it, but my creature spoke to me. 'Tell her that she must keep it.'

"I closed my mouth and said nothing at first. But by the end of the evening, I'd used persuasional skills that I wouldn't've guessed that I possessed to talk Vicky into keeping a baby that she most assuredly didn't want. Temporary parasite, indeed. Maybe she listened to me because I was older than her. Maybe she agreed because the bean-bug-baby inside her was communicating telepathically with her. I don't know.

"She told me that she thought she'd been careful, been safe. She said she had no idea who the father might be, and didn't feel like calling a meeting about it. She told me that she'd go ahead and have the baby, but she'd already made up her mind – I suspected that her mind might've been made up for her – that she'd give it up.

"I became Vicky's Lamaze coach, and by the time the baby was due, the voice in my head had instructed me: we'd already picked out a suitable adoptive mother, and all the arrangements had already been made.

"I went to the hospital with Vicky, all the time wondering what kind of monster she was going to deliver. But it was no monster. It was a perfect, nine pound, five ounce baby girl, with ten fingers and toes."

"Carly Dutch," I said.

"Yes," Cat replied.

So, according to this tale, I thought, *Carly wasn't the monster. The monster was inside her, genetically engineered.*

I said, "Did they kill Vicky? The aliens, I mean? Did they kill her? I remember you said she died in a car wreck."

Cat shrugged. "I don't know. Could be. I don't know why they would. They have a high regard for human women."

Except when they're filleting them like Caspian Sturgeon, I thought.

Cat continued. "But they could have. They can do anything."

Especially with your help, I thought.

Cat paused. She seemed to be considering the idea that her imaginary aliens had done away with their brood mare once they were through with her – like the thought had never crossed her mind before. I wondered if Cat herself had done away with Vicky.

After a moment, Cat said, "You've seen Carly's picture? Do you think that she looks like Sandy at all? 'Cause there might be a little of Sandy in her."

"I didn't notice a resemblance," I said.

I mulled over Cat's story – that little Carly Dutch, she of the pink room and the *Little Mermaid* DVD, was actually a genetically engineered mutant alien, equipped with castrating lady parts. I thought that the shrinks would be able to gnaw and chew on this one for years. There would be a website – at least one – and there'd be books and books and books written about it.

I asked, "Where is Carly now, Cat?"

"What we have at Zagairre," she said, not answering my question, "is a large community of girls like Carly. They're called second-wavers. Some were grown and raised entirely on the mother planet; these ones come off as a little foreign to me, which of course, is understandable. Some were implanted and raised by human families, like Carly. Each possesses the harvesting organ."

"Everyone at Zagairre is an alien?" I asked.

Cat smiled maternally at me, like she thought I might be simple. "No, Si, not everyone. There are many girls from fine families attending Zagairre, and they're all just as human as

127

you and me." She considered, then added with a wink, "Well, just as human as you.

"I'll admit that we'd like to phase them out, however. Someday, we'll have an all-alien student body – won't that be glorious? But we're not quite there yet. At this point, we still need the funding that the human girls provide.

"The alien women have seen to it that I've risen to a position of authority. Zagairre was once a stuffy finishing school for rich girls, something for them to do while they were waiting around to marry rich boys. The aliens and I have transformed it, guiding hirings and firings and retirements, until I'm its leader. They've entrusted me with the safety and welfare of the most important group of young women in their history. The most important group of young women in *our* history, for that matter.

"The second-wavers attend special classes. Of course, no one knows they're special classes, not even the second-wavers themselves. Do you understand, Si? Not even the off-worlders know what they have inside them. Their memories are hidden from them, new memories installed. They're instructed in their function subconsciously, telepathically. Then, when the time comes, all is revealed to them.

"We have fifteen sighted second-wavers at Zagairre – that's what we call the ones who know their purpose. They work as teachers' aides, mostly, until their college education is complete. Then they'll go out into the world. I'm so looking forward to the big conference, the day after tomorrow, Si! It'll be composed entirely of sighted second-wavers, from all over the world."

"This is an international thing?" I asked.

Cat smiled. "Our world is shot through with second-wavers, Si, all descended from those first five women and the testicles they harvested. All the sighted second-wavers on planet Earth are scheduled to gather here in two days. All of our eggs in one posh basket, so to speak. It's not a huge number, compared to the world's population, but there are a few, so we'll be meeting in the auditorium.

128

"It's Spring Break this week, so the human student body is mostly gone, as well as most of the non-sighted second-wavers. If any of the human students or non-sighted second-wavers that've remained are studious enough that they think they might want to attend our unannounced meeting, if they just happen to be passing by and see a bunch of their fellows standing around outside the auditorium beforehand, say – on the outside chance that that might happen – some of the sighted second-wavers standing guard outside the doors will gently but firmly turn them away. It's not like it'll be necessary to check names on a list, Si – it's not like anyone not initiated will be able to sneak in. No imposters will be able to slide through, because sighted second-wavers can identify each other. They can sense each other – they know each other on sight. Still, it won't do for any strangers to be here, snooping around.

"At the appointed time, those on guard will also gather inside. The lights will dim and Freya will appear and speak to us."

"Telepathically?" I asked.

"Of course. If anyone were to somehow get in then, it would look like we were all just meditating, or praying."

Except for the Darth Vader/Cthulhu woman in the cat suit leading the mantra, I thought. *She might stand out a little bit, what with the tentacles and all.*

"It's quite an honor for Zagairre to've been chosen for this conference," Cat was saying. "I like to look at it as a personal honor bestowed upon me as a reward for all my years of devoted service. It will be glorious!" She paused to bask in her glory, then said, "Now can you see why I'm telling you all this, Si? Can you see the importance of it all? When the second-wavers are at last called to their purpose –"

"And what exactly is their purpose, Cat?" I asked.

"Second-wavers are girls who've been engineered so that they possess the harvesting organ. But they cannot conceive. Their purpose, when they are called to it, will be to harvest. That's what they were created to do. After each has made a harvest, she'll then return to the mother planet. We couldn't

129

very well have them running around down here, where diligent police officers like you would eventually apprehend them for what they've done, now could we?

"Once they're on the home world, the testicles that they've harvested will be used to create the third wave. Third-wavers will not only be able to harvest, they'll also be able to conceive, to bear the first natural generation of the new, blended race!"

"And how will all that go, Cat? How will that blending work? Especially for human men?"

"Well, I guess it'll work just how you think, Si." Cat paused. "So far, they haven't been working too much on what the blended *boy* will be like. In fact, they haven't been working on that at all." She grinned wickedly. "Ya'll boys here on Earth are gonna work out just fine, just the way you are. Alien boys won't be necessary. Like I said, the alien women figure that if their men want to die out, let 'em die out. The third-wavers will harvest and conceive just like the original alien women did with their own men. Only they will be harvesting from human men, now.

"They'll conceive only girls: they've been designed to utilize only the girl sperms from human men. They'll come here, harvest, go back home, and raise their daughters. Whenever a group of them decides that they want to conceive again, they'll just get together and come back."

I repeated this insanity back to her. "So, the plan is for these women, who look just like regular women, to periodically prey on human men in order to propagate their species? Is that it, Cat? Like lionesses picking off a few stray zebras from the herd? Are you saying that in twenty years or so, the average guy won't be able to tell what he's taking to bed? He'll never know whether or not he might wake up a eunuch?"

Cat smiled. "I guess you could put it that way, Si. But it won't take twenty years. The fertile third-wavers will be here sooner than that. The sighted second-wavers are already here, and will be receiving their instructions at the conference."

She grinned in delight. "A few men are going to be waking up as eunuchs, worldwide – maybe as early as next week."

"What happens when one of your girls gets caught in the act?" I asked, going along completely with her insanity now, because I was curious to see just how fully formed and well-rounded her delusion actually was.

I used my imagination, my ever so useful imagination, and thought like a cop. I imagined another Sammy Mellucci sitting across from me in an interrogation room. I imagined him accused of first degree murder, because he'd killed some trick that'd cut his nuts off. I imagined exchanging glances with Solly, as we listened to the poor guy's now familiar story.

I imagined standing around at the girl's autopsy, imagined the look of amazed, delighted surprise on the face of the M.E. when he cut the body open and found all this new and different equipment. "Well, would you look at that!" he'd say. "There's something you don't see every day!"

I imagined that after the very first one was taken, either dead or alive, then the game would be up for these castrating alien bitches. Once the first one was discovered, means would be devised to detect them. Means would be devised to detect them *immediately.* Men just don't fuck around when it comes to the possible loss of these things. They'd rather lose an eye or an arm or a lung.

"What happens then, Cat?" I asked again. "When one of them gets caught? Do they have some kind of cyanide tooth to bite down on, or some way to disintegrate themselves? Because they can't afford to be letting themselves get caught, now can they? Once we find out – forewarned is forearmed and all that."

Cat smiled again. "No one is ever going to get caught, Si. By the time the third-wavers arrive – they'll be designed so that it'll all seem as natural as regular sex to you people – you men will never know what hit you. You'll wake up eunuchs, just like you said, and the girls will be gone. The whole process – seduction to sayonara – will be perfected with the third-wavers."

131

I dared to express doubt. "So you're saying there'll be no more misfires? Like with you and Sammy Mellucci?"

Cat blinked politely. "Me and who?"

"Sammy Mellucci. Your failed . . ." I was going to say *victim,* but thought better of it. "Your failed *conquest.* From the warehouse."

"Was that his name? Sammy? I suppose he would have a name, wouldn't he?" It was obvious from the look on her face that Cat had not given the man that she'd so gruesomely, so cavalierly maimed – she'd not given him so much as one single thought in all these years.

"Yes," I told her. "His name was Sammy Mellucci. He was no prince, not by a long shot, but you kinda screwed him for life, Cat. And I don't mean just physically." I restrained the urge to gesture at myself. No use directing her attention in that direction at this point in this insane conversation.

"Since they could never pin all those deaths on anyone else, and since every polygraph and test in the world that they gave Sammy showed that he believed that he was telling the God's honest truth when he said that octopus-faced women with ray guns had killed all his buddies, they've kept him locked up at State all these years. I don't even know if he's still alive, to tell you the truth. I didn't keep in touch with him, you see. Regardless, that's the only way he's ever gonna get out of there. In a box."

Again, Cat blinked politely. "I'm so sorry to hear that," she said, not sorry at all.

I thought about the depth of her icy emptiness, and then another thought struck me. I said, "You said that none of this second-wave harvesting has started yet?"

Cat nodded. "It won't begin until after the conference," she said.

"Except for Carly," I reminded her. "Why was Carly *called to her purpose* already? Was she a test case or something?"

Cat sighed; her shoulders drooped dejectedly. "Carly's harvest was a mistake. A *misfire,* as you put it."

132

I waited for further explanation.

"Carly is only fourteen years old, Si. She was still blind, unaware of the differences in her body. Her subconscious conditioning had only just begun. By the time she was sixteen or eighteen, she would've been made sighted, conscious – she would've been able to control the harvesting tentacle. But she's still just a baby. She wasn't even aware that it was there. Somehow, she went home, ran afoul of this rapist –"

"He's no rapist, Cat," I said. "He's just a kid that exercised poor judgment. He's old enough to've known better, but Carly had a crush on him. She's cute, took him by the hand. He only went as far as she let him. He didn't force her. He didn't rape anybody."

Cat's grin widened nastily. "He won't rape anybody ever again, will he?"

I let that remark and the stark truth of it slide right on by.

I repeated, "But what happens if there's a misfire like you and Sammy's again? Or what happens if the girl decides that she likes or even loves the dude, like Carly? Because that's what caused her misfire, wasn't it? She had feelings for Scott Holland. What happens if some second-waver decides that she likes the guy, maybe wants to stay with him – what if she decides that she doesn't want to cripple him for life?"

Cat sighed and smiled. "I think you're laboring under a couple of misconceptions, here, Si, so allow me to address these concerns of yours, one at a time. First, my *misfire,* as you so charmingly term it, was no doubt caused by the crude and primitive nature of the first-wave mechanical device. That problem has been addressed, done away with, rendered moot. The second-wavers have an organic device."

"Yet still there can be misfires," I insisted, fully entrenched in this fantastical scenario now, right there beside Cat in her madness, discussing all the angles of this crazy shit, just like it was the gospel truth. "Witness Carly and her affections."

"Like I told you before, Si, Carly was uninitiated. She didn't know what it is she possesses. Whether or not emotion or affection had anything to do with it – that's a phenomenon that the alien women will have to research. Carly's episode was a mistake – just like sex with any fourteen-year-old girl is undoubtedly a mistake. This mistake just had a little bit graver consequences for her partner." Again, Cat grinned nastily.

Then she said, "Had Carly been sighted . . . Let me explain a little something to you about this melding of the species, Si, about how sighted second-wavers are different from regular human girls their age – pretty much different from any other human girls of any age, for that matter.

"Even me – why do you think you're so drawn to me, Si? It's the alien influence. If I decide that I want some man, I can make myself irresistible to him. He becomes like the rat that decides he wants to fuck the cat. Despite his better judgment, he simply cannot help himself.

"Our sighted second-wavers have the same . . . *power*, if you will. To a man they want, they are irresistible. And unlike other girls, unlike myself – they have no emotions about the thing to gum up the works. They don't *fall in love* – at least not with human men. There might be a kind of affection, and they most certainly enjoy the act, probably more than human women might ever dream of enjoying it – but there's no more love involved than you might feel for a big, juicy hamburger. You anticipate, you enjoy – but the thought never crosses your mind not to eat it, based on some *emotion*. All the fun – the very point, in fact – is to *eat* that hamburger, right? The hamburger's thoughts and feelings don't enter into the picture, now do they?

"And so it is with second-wavers. The point is to have a good time, harvest some testicles – *eat that hamburger*. Then they get to go to the home world – and how exciting must the idea of that be for them? Once there, they'll turn over their harvests. Maybe come back, do it all again. Second-wavers can't conceive, but their equipment is reusable."

Cat paused, shrugged. "And if there are any misfires, if for some reason you men get hep to the aliens among you, then they'll just start abducting you and taking you back to the home world for the procedure, instead of completing it here.

"And since you men are, unfortunately, just one time use – as far as *these* women are concerned, anyway – and, as such, since you are of absolutely no value to them whatsoever after they've harvested what they want from you – maybe they'll just *eat you* when they're through. As if you really are that hamburger. Like black widows or praying mantises do. Or like Sirians supposedly do with their enemies." Cat winked.

It occurred to me that this whole elaborate delusion was really just an expression of Cat's misandry – her total hatred for men. In my somewhat limited experience with women, I'd never met any real man-haters, and surely nothing like this. Some women I knew hated one or two men in particular, individuals that they felt had done them wrong – but I'd never known any women that'd hated us all, as a *gender.* Not like this.

On the other hand, I know lots of men that hate women. Through and through. In fact, *most men* hate women, I've found. Liking sex doesn't equate to liking women, my friends. Lots of men enjoy sex with women, and still hate their guts. Sex is their only use – if they're not in bed with them, they find women annoying, stupid, superfluous.

But it always seemed to me that women who like men – regular gals, if you will – they like men all around, not just for sex. They want men for companionship – to be friends and protectors, in addition to being lovers. But Cat was certainly different – I'd never met a woman before that so obviously, so completely despised men the way Cat did, and yet still so obviously and so completely enjoyed having sex with them.

But then, on the other hand, Cat was just as crazy as a March hare. If I was unsure about anything else, I was completely convinced of that.

I was amazed at the lengths the subconscious mind could go to express emotions and motives that the conscious mind wouldn't admit to having. Because I was sure that if you asked Cat, she wouldn't say that she hated men. Right up until the

135

time that she'd yanked violently on my handcuffed arm and began this misandrist tale to end all misandrist tales, I certainly wouldn't've said that she hated *me*.

But she'd definitely loved Sandy, and maybe when Sandy came back to me, that'd just been too much for her. Maybe Cat had snapped, then, and all of this was just the elaborate construct of her diseased mind, her way of getting back at me and men in general for Sandy's leaving her behind and returning to the heterosexual fold.

"Where's Carly now?" I asked again.

"Carly's gone, Si. Somehow she found her way back here after the . . . *incident*. She was a mess, barefoot, blood-spattered, distraught, hysterical. I have no idea how she made it back here without someone seeing her. She said something about hitchhiking. I put her in the tub, then gave her a Valium and sent her to bed.

"In the morning a woman with tentacles arrived and took her home to the mother planet. I don't know if it was the same woman, if it was Freya. They all look alike, but –"

Now I was really amazed at the fullness of Cat's delusion. I asked, *"You saw a space ship?"*

Cat stopped pacing, looked at me in annoyance. "No, I didn't *see* a space ship! Do you think that they just landed on the commons in broad daylight? The woman came to collect her, and Carly left with her. They went out to the woods. I imagine the ship was parked out there."

And I imagined, with my ever-ready, crystal-clear imagination, that Carly was still out there in the woods, and that all it would take would be a cadaver dog to find her. And I imagined that an autopsy would show no extra alien organs. *Why hadn't this place been searched with dogs when she first disappeared?* I wondered. More shoddy police work.

Cat was staring steadily at me now, a mist of that smoky look returning to her eyes. I wanted to tell her, *No thank you, sister, my daddy always told me never to sleep with anyone crazier than I am.*

At last she spoke. "I suppose you're wondering why I've told you all of this, Si."

That was indeed the question of the hour, so I nodded.

"There are really several reasons. When I saw you today, you looked so sad and lost, and I realized it must've been hell on you all these years, not knowing why Sandy was sacrificed. Why she all of a sudden did all of those horrible things to attract strange men, why she ended up so horribly. I realized that I was the only one in the world that could relieve that pain for you, the pain of not knowing, of not understanding.

"I realized that it must've nearly killed you to see her like that. Not only dead, but surrounded by all that sordidness. I was the only one that could explain to you that the sordidness wasn't Sandy's fault. That it really hadn't been your Sandy that'd participated in all that, but someone who was being guided by a force that she didn't even know was there."

Yeah, I thought, *I'm completely relieved by this explanation, all right.*

"Secondly, since I told you about the first part, I wanted you to know about Carly. Now you can quietly drop your investigation, or maybe just drop out of it, however those police things work. *Because Carly is gone,* Si. She's realized her destiny a little early, and is right now on another world. She won't be coming back here, I don't think. The experience was quite traumatic for her, because she wasn't yet properly conditioned for it. Regardless, there's no reason to continue to waste the taxpayers' money looking for her, because if she does come back, it won't be for a long time.

"And of course, I can't have you running around here turning over rocks, looking for a girl who is a million light years away, when the delegation is going to be here in two days. How would that look? They'd never let me host another important function!"

Now Cat turned and dropped her robe to the floor. "But the most important reason," she said as she climbed astride me again, "the most important reason I told you all of this, Si, is that I'm lonely. I'm not emotionless about men, like a second-waver. I've missed you, all of these years. I was wondering if you might like to be my . . . boyfriend."

I'm sorry, ladies and gentlemen, but at that point, I could not restrain my guffaw. I laughed right out loud, right in her face.

But before her feelings could be hurt, before she could perhaps become angry at me for laughing at her, I said quickly, still going along with her delusion, "Gee, I don't know, Cat. I'd kinda like to keep my balls. And my dick."

A thundercloud had gathered on her brow when I'd laughed at her, but now it departed. "Oh! You're concerned about my little friend! Has it hurt you yet? Not at all. In fact, it has been instrumental in making ours the best sex you've ever had.

"We are symbiotic, it and I, Si. Its original function has been forgotten. It's become quite happy where it is. It realizes that if it was to complete its original function now, the women would take it home and destroy it to process your testicles. So it would never hurt you. In fact, I think it rather likes you."

Cat was squatting over me now, and when she looked down at herself, I followed her gaze and watched in utter, amazed horror as a metallic *thing* snaked out of her. It was about as thick as my thumb and looked a little like braided cable. But there was only a passing resemblance to anything manufactured: the thing pulsed and moved and was patently alive.

A serrated edge slid out of its end and then slid back in, as if it was demonstrating for me how it *could* hurt me, but was assuring me that it *wouldn't*. I closed my eyes, thinking I had to be hallucinating. But when I opened them again, it was still there, uncoiling slowly, traveling inexorably downward toward me.

I don't know if you can imagine yourself in a similar situation, or imagine how you might react if you found yourself in a situation such as that. I'll make it easy for you. I reacted the same way you would if someone threw a big, hairy spider on you: I screamed, and drove my right knee upward; Cat fell forward onto my chest, and I shoved her hard, off of me, with my left hand.

Then with the index finger of my left hand, I reached over and released the catch on Solly's trick handcuffs, leapt off the bed, grabbed my gun and pointed in at Cat, who was now lying on the floor, her legs crossed demurely. The braided cable or whatever it was, was no longer visible.

Oh, wait. You didn't really think that I'd actually allow this crazy bitch to incapacitate me, did you? *Oh, hell, no!* No, no, no!

The first lesson I learned at Papa Nova's knee had been: "If some girl's kinky enough to want to handcuff you, she's kinky enough to do anything, including cut your nuts off."

How prophetic that turn of phrase turned out to be.

"But," Solly had continued, "she might not be that kinky after all, so it might be fun to go with it. There's a lot of ground that can be covered between fun and dangerous." He'd then presented me with the trick cuffs, and said, "Enjoy!"

I was panting, pointing my gun at Cat. I was on one side of the bed and she was on the floor on the other side. We were both naked. She arose slowly, gracefully, and gathered up her robe and put it on. She looked at the handcuff key on the night table, looked at me, then leaned over the bed and unhooked the handcuffs from the headboard via the other hidden catch.

She held the cuffs out to me. I snatched them from her and backed away. Now I felt stupid, with handcuffs in one hand and a gun in the other, panting, afraid, still naked.

I gestured with the gun. "That *thing,*" was all I could say.

She smiled. "What thing, Si?"

"That thing, inside you. What is it? What kind of trick is this?"

Cat sighed. "I just told you the whole story, Si. I'm guessing from your reaction that the boyfriend thing is out of the question. I knew that it was probably impossible, but I had to ask. I've always been so fond of you, Si. I realize now that the idea of . . . of *sharing* that particular space with something else is probably just a little bit more than you can handle." She sighed again. "I'm going to go over here and lay face down on the bed, and put my hands behind my head, so you can feel safe while you put your clothes on. But then, I'll have to insist that you leave, because I think our date is over."

Cat did what she said she was going to do and I quickly put the cuffs down and gathered up my clothes in one hand, still holding the gun on her. I threw on my pants and shirt, never putting the gun down. It was quite an accomplishment, let me tell you.

Cat, her voice muffled by the bed, said, "No one's going to believe you, if you start blabbing about what I've told you, Si."

It wasn't that I believed that she had a sentient, alien creature living inside her. But there was definitely something in there. I thought that maybe Cat's insanity was more sophisticated than I'd first realized – maybe she'd had the thing surgically implanted somehow, like those people that have lumps of metal inserted under their skin to resemble horns. Or maybe it was just lodged in there somehow. What do I know about women's anatomies, what they could hold in there? I knew that they could smuggle things.

Then a vicious thought struck me, and I grinned humorlessly: surgically installed or otherwise, I bet it would come right on out of there if I yanked hard enough on it. It was not at all a pretty sentiment, but I have to admit that I did enjoy ruminating on it. Tearing that thing out of her wouldn't cause anything as monstrous as the pain that Sandy and the other girls had endured, but it would be a start. And while I could never actually have done such a thing, I'm not ashamed to admit that I did enjoy thinking about it.

I said, "I'll have you brought in. Make you get an x-ray."

"Nothing will show on an x-ray, Si. Did you feel anything? No. That's because it's part of me now, part of my tissue." She propped her head up on one elbow, keeping the other hand behind her head. "No one will believe you, Si."

I had my shoes, holster, and the trick handcuffs in one hand, and my gun in the other. I gave up my socks and shorts as lost. "You just lay there until you hear my car drive away.

I'm not entirely sure what's going on here, Cat. All I know is that I'm completely freaked out, and I wouldn't want to have to shoot you. I have to talk to my partner about all this crazy shit," I added absently.

"You don't need to talk to anyone, Si," Cat said sharply. "You just need to go home and think about it, and then you need to just decide to keep it all to yourself. I'm warning you. Bad things will happen if you start spouting all sorts of craziness about this!" I backed out of the room and down the stairs. "Bad things!" Cat shouted after me. "I can't have you screaming all sorts of ridiculous stories while the delegation is here! I'm not going to let you ruin my big day, Si! You just keep your goddamn mouth shut! Or I promise, you will be sorry!"

I snatched my jacket off the chair where I'd left it and fled the house like the very hounds of hell were after me, jumped in the car, and didn't stop until I was at the bottom of the hill away from Zagairre School. I'd like to say that I pulled over and puked, but I'm a cop, after all, and I have a very strong stomach. So nothing as dramatic as all that happened.

I did pull over, however, to collect my thoughts and put my shoes on. It was all too much to assimilate at once. I still couldn't buy the alien, sentient, robot testicle-harvester idea, although that alive-looking tentacle thing had freaked me the hell out for a minute. I'd heard stories about girls in Mexico who could pick up dimes. I reasoned that maybe somehow Cat could manipulate that cable thing with her muscles, make it move like it was alive.

My cell rang. It was Solly. I pushed the button, and started with, "Dude, you are not going to believe this –"

But he cut me off. "Whatever it is, I got you beat, my friend, eight ways to Sunday. I just called to say that I saw your car parked out in front of the Director's house earlier this evening. You're a very bad boy, partner."

"You saw my car? How'd you know it was the Director's house?" I asked.

"That's what I called to tell you about. Remember, I had a fender bender this morning? Turns out this babe is some kind of student teacher or something, right there at the Zagairre School. Says she knows Miss Catarina and everything. It's a small world after all, right? She's the one who told me it was the Director's house that you were parked out in front of, you sly dog."

I heard a rushing in my ears. Cat screamed, *Bad things!* in my head. *You will be sorry!*

I yelled, "Solly! You gotta listen to me. Are you still here? At Zagairre?"

"No, I'm at my place now. We've been here all day, actually, since our little accident this morning. Except for when she made me drive her all the way up there earlier – she said she had to pick up some makeup or some other girlie stuff. She *insisted* that she had to go get it, so how could I tell her no? It's a long drive, but she made it worth my while on the way. That's when I saw your car. We've only been back here a little while. She's out on the balcony right now, talking on the phone, so I thought I'd give you a call and tell you what's up. Except for that drive up there and back, it's like the first break I've had from her all day.

"Oh, my God, Si, this girl! I don't usually like 'em this young, you know that. But that's because they're just so dumb when they're this young, and they don't have a clue as to what they're doing. But this one – she can't be a day over nineteen – the things she does! I think I'm in love! Or at least parts of me are in love."

I felt like things were moving in slow motion, like in one of those dreams where you're trying to get somewhere, but every imaginable circumstance keeps preventing you from achieving your goal.

Solly was an exceptional cop – he was a flawless interrogator, an inventive, imaginative, thorough-going detective. Yesterday, he'd even been willing to examine my admittedly off-the-wall pet theory that there had to be more than just a coincidence afoot here – there had to be some connection between Carly, the new castration suspect, and Cat, the original one.

But Sol was way more the ladies' man than he was the cop, at least right this minute. He'd been willing to look at things my way, to draw a connection between Carly and Cat – he hadn't been *all that willing*, actually, but he'd been willing enough to make an appointment to come over here and talk to Cat about it.

But the idea of drawing a line from long ago death and mutilation, through Carly and Cat, and then right on through to some friendly young thing that also happened to attend Zagairre School was something he was just not prepared to do. I could tell that Sol was completely relaxed, at his ease – not in the least bit suspicious of this apparently random interaction with a member of the student body from the same school that he was investigating.

I wanted to reach through the phone and shake him. "Sol," I shouted. "Did she make a call or did someone call her?"

"What?" he asked.

I gritted my teeth and tried to be calm, tried to talk slowly. This was no time to panic. Maybe it was all just a coincidence, after all.

They can do anything, Cat said in my head. *They have no emotions about the thing to gum up the works.*

I lowered my voice in an effort to project calm. I had to communicate to Sol, as directly as possible, that he was in grave danger. Let him laugh at me, let him say I was crazy – but if I told him that he was in danger, he would at least *hear me*, even if he didn't necessarily *believe me*. He'd at least consider what I was saying, and put his guard up.

I said, "Listen to me carefully, Sol. The girl. The phone call she's on. Did she call someone, or did someone call her?"

"What?" he asked again.

"Just answer the question, for Christ's sake." I repeated it for him. "Did she call someone, or did someone call her?"

"Someone called her. We were going at it for like the eleventh time today, and her phone rang. She jumped up – said she had to answer it. Said she was sorry, but she just had to take it. She's standing out on the balcony in my shirt right now, still on the phone.

Still in slow motion, I said, "Solly, you've got to listen to me –"

But a silky female voice cut me off. "Detective Nova can't talk any more right now." Then she giggled. "He probably won't call you back later." I heard Solly laugh and the call ended.

I dialed his number again, and it went straight to voicemail. I called Cat's number, too, trying to get her to call it off, but she didn't answer either. I raced back up the hill to the *Director's Residence.* The house was dark and quiet. I pounded on the door. No response. She might be still inside, but she might not be. She could be anywhere on campus by now, or she could've already left. It was fruitless to try and find her.

The feeling of helplessness, of inevitability, nearly crushed me. I got on the radio and called it in. I told the dispatcher that I'd been talking to my partner on the phone and I thought I'd heard a gunshot, and then the phone went dead.

I put the flasher on the dashboard, just like on TV, and sped down the freeway. When I got to Solly's place a half an hour later, it was like déjà vu. The tape was already up. An ambulance was parked nearby, no lights on, as dark and silent as the tomb.

I was on foreign soil once again. Sol lived just outside of our jurisdiction, so I didn't know any of the cops that were there. Again. But I knew that no lifelong friendship was gonna spring from this crime scene. Not this time.

Nervelessly, I took out my badge and hung it around my neck. I walked up the steps to Solly's second floor apartment, stepped through the tape, walked into his bedroom.

Solly was on his back, blue eyes open, staring at the ceiling. He was naked, and he looked quite surprised. As I stood there, someone covered him with a sheet. It was probably too soon, all the pictures probably hadn't been taken from all the possible angles. But someone in charge had decided that enough was enough. He was a fellow cop, after all. They had some respect.

Before the merciful sheet fell and covered my only friend in the world, I was not surprised to see that he hadn't been castrated. No, that would've just drawn more attention to the whole thing: homicide detective investigating castration gets castrated. And that's just what Cat didn't want, more attention. So, no castration.

Instead, Solly's throat had been slit most thoroughly, from ear to ear. Whoever'd murdered him had written *Maybe now you'll keep quiet* on the wall behind his head with his blood.

I heard one of the uniforms say to his buddy, "Yeah, he's gonna keep quiet now. He's gonna keep quiet forever."

But they had it all wrong. The bloody message wasn't for Sol, didn't really even concern him. The words scrawled on the wall in my friend's blood were for me.

A detective came up and looked at me. He said, "You're his partner? You called it in?"

I turned to him in surprise. "Yeah. How'd you know?"

He shrugged. "I knew you weren't one of ours. What happened?"

I told him the same lie I'd told the dispatcher – that I'd been talking to Sol on the phone. "He said, 'Someone's here.' I thought I heard a shot after that, and then the phone went dead."

"No one else heard any gunfire," the detective told me, a shade of suspicion in his voice. He nodded at my partner's corpse. "He wasn't shot."

I shrugged. "Cellphones. Maybe I didn't hear a shot at all. It was mostly his tone when he said, 'Someone's here,' that worried me."

"Any ideas who could've done it?" he asked.

I shook my head. I knew exactly who'd done it, or more accurately, who'd ordered it done. The *girlie stuff* that she'd had to get was probably the knife. I wondered vaguely if she'd cleaned the room. I doubted it – her fingerprints had to be everywhere, her DNA all over Solly. I wondered if Cat would make her disappear now, too, just like Carly Dutch. Because if she didn't disappear, these cops from Solly's town would surely catch her. Wouldn't they?

Poor Solly. My best friend, the ladies' man. In all his born days, I bet he never would've imagined that he'd get it like this, from some nineteen-year-old girl, right in the middle of the act. The thing in life that'd always come so easily to him.

I thought that to me – or to any other guy in his mid-forties – the whole thing would've seemed to be a set-up, right from the beginning. I would've been immediately suspicious when a beautiful nineteen-year-old-girl came on to me, would've wondered what the catch was. It would've all seemed just a little too good to be true to me, and I might've kept my hand on my wallet, on my gun – I might've been a little extra cautious.

And once I'd found out that she went to Zagairre, that she knew Miss Catarina, I would've been doubly suspicious. I would never have turned my back on such a girl.

But not Solly. That kinda thing happened to him all the time, young girls propositioning him. It was old news. He wouldn't've seen a single ulterior motive in this girl's attention. He knew what she wanted – he knew what *they all wanted*. He didn't hold their obvious desire against them, and he had absolutely no compunctions whatsoever about giving them what they wanted.

This was the one thing, good cop or not, that he never would've seen coming.

What a way to go, I thought. *Poor Sol.*

"Where were you for the last two hours or so?" the detective asked.

I wasn't offended. It was just police work. "For the last half-hour or so, I was driving over here. Before that, for the last several hours, I was having dinner with a friend," I told him. "I'm sure she'll vouch for me."

The detective nodded, said, "I'm sorry about your partner."

Feeling like a dime store Sam Spade, I said, "Yeah. So am I."

So I guess the rest of the story pretty much tells itself.

I went back home, and called Cat. She answered on the first ring, now. "I got your message, Cat," I told her. "I'll keep my mouth shut."

"I'm sorry it had to come to this, Si," she said softly. "But you left me no choice. If you would've just stayed with me for a little while longer, we could've talked it all out."

"How did you know where to find my partner?" I asked.

"His name was on my calendar, remember? He was supposed to be the one coming to see me this morning, not you. When I saw this cop's name on my calendar, yesterday afternoon, I sent young Nicole down to the police station. She's my favorite sighted second-waver. My protégé, you might say.

"Nicole got somebody to point this Detective Solomon Nova out to her, on the down low. Then she followed him, arranged to have that little accident with him this morning.

"The plan was just to have her distract him for a few days, until after the delegation. After that, I would've answered any questions that he had for me. But no one counted on *you* showing up, Si. And then, after I told you everything, I was so sure that you'd go along with me. I never would've thought that a good cop like you would've freaked out and ran off like you did.

"But I couldn't take any chances that you'd start blabbing. So I called Nicole, and told her what she had to do. It's your fault, Si. You got your partner killed. I couldn't have you running around –"

"Yeah, when the alien delegation is in town. I know," I cut her off, then said, "Some cops might come out and speak to you, 'cause I told them I was with you tonight. You're my alibi."

She tittered prettily. "I'll vouch for you."

I told her thanks and hung up. Then I took a long, hot shower and thought it all over.

Cat had murdered Solly because she thought I was a coward like she was. She thought that seeing my friend with a Columbian necktie would scare me into silence, for fear that the same thing would happen to me, just like seeing Sandy and the rest of her friends dead had turned her into a traitor to the human race. Or however the whole thing had played out in her sick mind.

And for what? For what had she murdered my friend? It was all so her big day would go smoothly, so the aliens would marvel at what a good little traitor she was. Again, all in her diseased mind.

Because I still didn't believe that there were any aliens. Not a single one. But I believed that *Cat* believed there were aliens, and as *there is nothing either good or bad, but thinking makes it so,* she was just as dangerous as if it *were* so.

But I'm not afraid of her and her homicidal delusions. Just like those infected rats, I'm not afraid of anything, now. Not anymore.

If Cat hadn't killed Solly, things would've turned out differently. I would've gone to the boss, and quietly, rationally explained Cat's delusions to him. Then I would've quietly, rationally went back to the exclusive Zagairre School and arrested her, brought her in. At worst, the publicity might've gotten her fired, if nothing substantial could be proven. At best, they might've locked her up in the nuthouse, right there next to Sammy Mellucci, if he was still alive. His ensuing freak-out might've been enough corroboration to keep Cat there at State indefinitely, just like him. Maybe. Maybe not. It would've been worth the effort, if for no other reason than to disgrace her crazy ass.

But Cat did kill Solly, and now, thanks to her, I've only got one thing left in this life, so I'm not even afraid of dying. Maybe you could say that Cat's influence has turned me suicidal, like those worms driving the grasshoppers to drown themselves.

What's that one thing that I've got left, you ask? Oh, that would be *vengeance.*

I could try to pin Solly's murder on Cat. Wouldn't that make things tense around her precious School for a while? A homicide investigation, in full swing? But Cat's connection to

Solly's death was tenuous at best, and I'd have to bring up all her craziness to even begin to make that connection. And I was sure that her minion was long gone by now. A homicide investigation might mess up the alien delegation in Cat's delusion, but I was pretty sure that in the end, she'd skate on the murder charge.

So I'd made my own plans for making her pay for her crimes. Cat had laid it all out for me, helped formulate this plan in my mind. She and the other crazy women would be meeting at Zagairre in two days. Like I say, I still don't believe the whole alien fantasy, but I do believe in mass hypnosis and cults.

It was obvious that Cat hadn't acted alone in any of this. She couldn't've done that warehouse job by herself, and besides, Sammy had seen her accomplices. And she'd admitted to having one of her minions do Solly.

So I'm figuring that everyone that's going to be in that auditorium is a *true believer*, and therefore, just as crazy and just as deadly as Cat is.

They might not be from another planet, but they're dangerous, are they not, Cat and her cronies? Had they not somehow brainwashed Carly Dutch into castrating the first boy unlucky enough to have a go at her? Not to mention the one that'd wielded the knife on my poor, dead partner?

Hadn't they killed those five guys? And Pat, Billy, Taylor, and Chris? *And Sandy?*

They might not be aliens, but they're most assuredly murderers, most assuredly toxic to any man that they might decide has to go. So I've decided that *they have to go.*

Since there's not a jury in the world that'll convict Cat of anything based on whatever evidence I might produce, she'll never see the inside of a prison. And now, since I've decided that State is also too good for her, I figure it's time for a little good ol' American vigilante justice.

You agree with me, don't you, gentle listener? You agree that in the name of justice, I really have no other choice?

It didn't take much to wire the auditorium. After all the evenings I spent at my father's knee, I could've done it in my sleep. But it won't just be little harmless lights going off this time, no sirree.

And I guess they'll have to revisit security procedures at the Unit's depot after this. Even though they once kidded me, called me *gutless,* once – it was way too easy for me to just waltz in there and distract my old teammates long enough to relieve them of enough Detasheet to erase Zagairre's auditorium. Like it had never even been built.

Sorry, fellas. I wasn't yellow. I was in love.

And what more fitting end for the mad bomber than to go up with his bombs? I only wish that I could see Cat's face, only wish there was some way to make sure that she knows it was me that ruined her big day, in the worst possible way. I wish there was some way to allow her to feel her disgrace before she dies, so she can know what a failure she's been, in every way. She even failed at her own delusion, at being a traitor to the human race.

But I'd never do anything so melodramatic. I'd never risk getting caught for an ideal. If I let Cat see me, there could be a chance, however slim, that she might be able to stop me. So, I'll just have to be satisfied with her being dead, for all of them, *all of us,* just being dead.

No, no big reveal of betrayal for Batman and Catwoman. Just a big boom.

There's no one left for me to say good-bye to, so I'll just say good-bye, and send this thing.

Good-bye.

*****

Also by LM Foster

A Passing Resemblance
Contrariwise – A Tale of Twins
Corvino
Duck Feet
Two Green Keys

One Wilde Ride Trilogy:
Book One: It Might Have Been
Book Two: An Exceptional Boy
Book Three: What Should Never Be

Stars and Guitars:
Talk To a Movie Star
Where The Guitars Play

Tom and Wiley:
This Carnival of Strange
Wiley Royce
Generally Recognized as Safe
Wiley Royce Versus The Martians